A BRUSH WITH THE PAST

1900–1950

The years that changed our lives

Shirley Hughes

The Bodley Head
London

A BRUSH WITH THE PAST
A BODLEY HEAD BOOK 0 370 32839 6

Published in Great Britain by The Bodley Head,
an imprint of Random House Children's Books

This edition published 2005

1 3 5 7 9 10 8 6 4 2

Set in Berkeley Book

RANDOM HOUSE CHILDREN'S BOOKS
61–63 Uxbridge Road, London W5 5SA
A division of The Random House Group Ltd

RANDOM HOUSE AUSTRALIA (PTY) LTD
20 Alfred Street, Milsons Point, Sydney,
New South Wales 2061, Australia

RANDOM HOUSE NEW ZEALAND LTD
18 Poland Road, Glenfield, Auckland 10, New Zealand

RANDOM HOUSE (PTY) LTD
Endulini, 5A Jubilee Road, Parktown 2193, South Africa

THE RANDOM HOUSE GROUP Limited Reg. No. 954009
www.kidsatrandomhouse.co.uk

A CIP catalogue record for this book is available from the British Library.

Printed in Singapore

Contents

To my grandchildren
Paul, Adam, Jack, Alice, Elsa, Martha and Claudia

Introduction

The pictures I have painted for this book are full of ordinary people. They inhabit the first half of the twentieth century, that era of unprecedented social change when a great rush of invention and new technology impacted on everyone's life. I found that I could create all these imaginary scenes from my own memories of the 1930s onwards and from the old photograph albums, picture postcards, magazine illustrations and fashion advertisements which littered my childhood and exercised such a powerful fascination for me, as they still do.

Observant readers will notice that all my colour spreads show people having a meal of one sort or another. But the interest for me is not what they are eating but the drama of the occasion. Meals have always offered the artist's eye far more than merely a pleasing still life or figure composition. They often set the scene for a family confrontation or an intimate exchange of confidences, a plot, a celebration, a romance or even a battlefield. Whether eaten alone or in company, outside or in, served with pomp or the utmost informality, they tell you a great deal about the era in which they are taking place as well as the people who are gathered together.

I have not attempted to describe in my accompanying pages the great political upheavals, wars, famines, migrations and persecutions in any proper historical manner. But as my research for the black and white illustrations gathered momentum I found that each decade was illuminated by all sorts of information and images, from the momentously political to the decoratively trivial, a kind of mosaic which all seemed to hang together.

There is a wealth of history in crockery, hats, clothes, furniture and domestic appliances, not to mention sport, science and the arts. I hope that in picking over the clutter it will be possible to find, as I did, your own way into history. The pictures in this book are merely a starting point. The stories are all yours.

Shirley Hughes

Below stairs – London – 1900

Better-off homes had the luxury of a coal fire in the main rooms.

Fireplaces had to be cleaned out, swept and a new fire lit every morning before the family got up.

Britain, America and Germany were the biggest coal-producing countries in the world.

As coal mining grew, so did the steel works, creating three gigantic industrial powers.

The Brownie Box camera went on sale in the USA.

Photography was now within the reach of eager amateurs.

Pit boys as young as 13 worked in mines alongside the men, and took their dinner underground.

1900

I found it very easy to re-create a London basement kitchen at the turn of the century. I live in this kind of Victorian terrace house and, although the basements in our street are now mostly opened up into spacious kitchen-dining areas, the structure of ours remains much the same.

Kitchens then tended to be dominated by a cook and a cast-iron cooking 'range' which also supplied hot water. Unlike the grand 'upstairs, downstairs' households so familiar from television, which employed many servants of both sexes, with their own complicated pecking order, a middle-class home such as this would probably have employed two or three 'live-in' domestics, all female.

The lowliest person in this household was the scullery maid or 'tweeny', a teenage girl, often isolated and homesick, who slept in an unheated attic shared with another servant. The kitchen at least was warm – in summer unbearably hot – and the cook's temper was often correspondingly short.

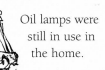

Oil lamps were still in use in the home.

Women suffered the agony of tightly laced corsets to achieve the desired 'hourglass' figure.

Towns and cities were still full of horse-drawn vehicles and lit by gas lamps.

The first underground electric railway had just opened in London.

In Vienna, Austria, designers and architects like Otto Wagner were breaking with the old ornate tradition and inventing an original, modern style.

Dr Sigmund Freud published *The Interpretation of Dreams*.

Followers of the Arts and Crafts movement in interior, textile and furniture design adopted a looser, more flowing style of dress.

Veils, goggles and dustcoats were worn by motorists.

Motor cars were still a novelty on the road.

There were many households without bathrooms. Hot water was carried upstairs. An average household used a fraction of what we waste today.

Hip baths, china washing bowls, chamber pots and slop pails all had to be emptied by hand.

Hats were worn everywhere.

They signified what social class you came from.

Hats like cartwheels, top hats, straw hats, hats with feathers, woolly hats, felt hats and 'deerstalker' hats with earflaps.

At work, the foreman showed his rank by wearing a bowler hat while his workmen wore cloth caps.

In ordinary homes, keeping the family clean was hard work.

The tweeny assisted the cook and the parlour maid. She helped prepare vegetables, carried coal upstairs from the coal cellar, laid fires, emptied slops, polished endless brass, scrubbed doorsteps and, of course, washed up.

Time off for an evening visit to church was allowed on Sundays and a half-day off a week was considered reasonable. Male admirers were strictly forbidden, though tradesmen delivering to the back door were known to linger for a chat or a little flirtation on the quiet.

Above stairs, a young wife's duty was to supervise domestic staff, to hire and fire, order meals, entertain and see that the home ran smoothly for her husband. It was an awesome and often lonely responsibility.

There was no shortage of domestic labour. For women it was a major source of employment, in many ways preferable to factory work. Women often continued to work after marriage and did all their own household chores too.

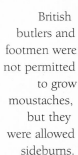

Parlour maids wore a cotton print dress in the mornings and changed into a black dress and a smart apron to wait on the family in the afternoons.

British butlers and footmen were not permitted to grow moustaches, but they were allowed sideburns.

Many households made do with a primitive outdoor toilet – a 'privy' – which was shared with the neighbours.

Washing up in a stone sink, with a hand-pumped cold-water tap.

Infection of food from flies was a big problem.

Refrigeration was in its early stages. Food was kept in a cool larder on slate shelves, carefully covered.

Breakfast in the haymeadow – New Hampshire – 1902

The English upper class traditionally enjoyed fox-hunting and shooting game.

The new king, Edward VII, was a keen sportsman.

US president Theodore (Teddy) Roosevelt, a renowned game hunter, on one occasion refused to shoot a bear.

Soon after this a toy store put a stuffed bear in the window, labelled 'Teddy's Bear'.

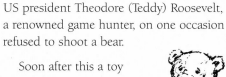

A long-lasting toy character had been invented.

The gamekeeper and the poacher were long-standing enemies.

Poached game often subsidized the family diet.

About 50% of land in the British Isles was owned by landlords.

Most farm labourers lived in 'tied' cottages on the landlord's property.

They had to leave when their employment ended. Old folk were sometimes allowed to remain, courtesy of the landlord.

The working dog then, as now, played a vital part in country life.

Country children had serious responsibilities, tending animals, not as pets, but as an important part of the family income.

People could not afford to be sentimental.

The family pig was fattened on scraps until it was time for it to be slaughtered.

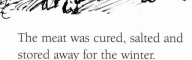

1902

There was still plenty of countryside around the north of England seaside town where I grew up, though it was already patchy with suburban development. But the proper country, I thought, was the one I read about in storybooks. It was the landscape of southern England, permanently bathed in sunshine, with thatched cottages set in pretty gardens full of wallflowers and hollyhocks, surrounded by cornfields and bosky woodland.

The land of storybook America appeared even more glamorous – a place of clapboard houses and barns, white picket fences, big skies and delicious home cooking; the setting for *Pollyanna* and *Rebecca of Sunnybrook Farm*. It seems odd now that, apart from the immortal Huck Finn, I barely encountered the hard side of rural life through the fictional eyes of a black or Native American child, for instance, or one from a poor sharecropping family.

Milkmaids carried buckets on wooden yokes across their shoulders.

The meat was cured, salted and stored away for the winter.

Killing the pig was a family celebration.

Standards of hygiene in milk production were not as high as they are today.

Milk was transported in metal milk churns, usually by cart, to the nearest railway station, and on to towns.

Daring 'new women' dressed for bicycling.

With the development of transport, rural communities became less isolated.

Social horizons widened, allowing a broader choice of mate.

Shirts, dresses and woollens, usually home-made, were carefully mended and patched.

Even the smallest off-cuts of material were made into patchwork quilts, sunbonnets or baby clothes.

Rural wifely skills also included bee-keeping. Honey was a valuable substitute for sugar.

Still the romance of these stories, so much enjoyed then, lingers. The hay meadow scene in my picture is somewhat idyllic, though in the year in which it is set, 1902, slavery was still very much within living memory. And already the old ways of farming were being radically changed in the USA and all over Europe by the impact of newly invented agricultural machinery.

As ancient country traditions began to disappear, so urban nostalgia for rural life increased. The town dweller, forgetting the hard drudgery of work on the land, yearned for the simple outdoor life. There was a growing urban interest in preserving folksongs and dances and rural crafts.

The American cowboy was already being mythologized in touring Wild West shows in which battles with 'Red Indians' in full war paint were re-enacted.

Some areas were slow to change – scything and reaping by hand continued.

Black children in the southern states of the USA could only attend school if they were not needed to work in the fields.

Girls in most poor families looked after the younger children while their mothers worked.

Horses had not yet been replaced by machinery.

Early pop-music promoters sold the latest song sheets.

All kinds of pedlars and purveyors of quack medicines toured the country fairs.

Cheap imported goods as well as local produce were offered on weekly market stalls.

The general store or village shop was a focal point in every rural community for gossip as well as shopping. It usually also served as a post office.

A picnic by the river – England – 1904

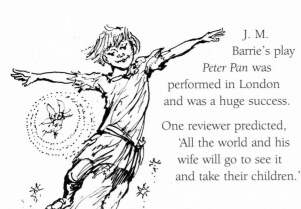

J. M. Barrie's play *Peter Pan* was performed in London and was a huge success.

One reviewer predicted, 'All the world and his wife will go to see it and take their children.'

In the USA Louis Comfort Tiffany developed a method of glass-blowing which produced a magical, light-filled effect.

Women protected their pale complexions from the sun with hats and parasols.

A suntan was not considered attractive, being associated with outdoor, manual labour.

It was fashionable to keep young babies in long, elaborate clothes which restricted movement.

Italian tenor Enrico Caruso made his first recording in the USA.

Giacomo Puccini's opera *Madame Butterfly* flopped at its première in Milan.

In France Pathé Frères launched their first regularly updated newsreels. They owned a chain of cinemas and showed films of exciting events such as the first powered flight, achieved by the Wright brothers in 1903.

1904

A picnic has always been a favourite subject for a painting. My 1904 town dwellers, dressed in their Sunday best, are enjoying a day out by the river, each in their own way.

City air was becoming more and more polluted by smoke from domestic and factory chimneys. People wanted to get out of their cramped tenements and back-to-back houses with doors opening directly onto the street. They dreamed of a neat suburban villa with a garden back and front and all the modern conveniences within: better cooking arrangements and bathrooms with hot and cold running water.

Suburban development was spreading at an unparalleled rate. People could now travel to and from work by train, tram or motor bus. Transport companies were hotly competing to open up these services. Even those who could not afford holidays might manage a day trip to the country.

Sea bathing was known to be healthy, but swimwear favoured extreme modesty!

Mixed bathing (men and women together) was accepted in France but only slowly in Britain.

Wooden bathing huts were wheeled to the water's edge for the convenience and privacy of bathers.

In the USA the World Fair in St Louis, Missouri, attracted huge crowds in very hot weather.

Ice-cream vendors hit on the idea of cone-shaped ice-cream holders made of waffles.

They did a roaring trade!

With improved colour printing, beautiful books were being produced.

Fairy tales, legends and classics were superbly illustrated by artists like Arthur Rackham, N. C. Wyeth, Edmund Dulac and W. Heath Robinson.

In the USA Theodore Roosevelt won a four-year term as president.

He wanted to protect the American wilderness.

150 million acres of US government timberland were set aside as forest reserve. National parks doubled. Wild bird sanctuaries were created.

Russian playwright Anton Chekhov's last play *The Cherry Orchard* was first performed in Moscow. He was too ill to attend.

He died later that year.

Beaded light shades were fashionable. So were Japanese lanterns and ceramics.

In Russia the Grand Siberian Railway was completed: 4,607 miles of track from the Ural Mountains to Vladivostok.

It had more than 1,000 stations and would open up Siberia and boost trade with China and the East.

Jack London's novel *The Sea Wolf* was published. It described the tough, brutal life on a seal-hunting schooner.

In Paris an exhibition of primitive African art excited young artists like Picasso.

This was an era of improved leisure and higher expectations. A rising class of 'white-collar' workers were eager for self-improvement. They took night classes, correspondence courses and used public libraries. In the USA one of the first concerns of a newly arrived immigrant was to learn English.

A whole new reading public was developing. People devoured newsprint, adventure stories, westerns, detective thrillers and romances. Press barons like Northcliffe and Beaverbrook in Britain and Hearst in the USA were quick to cater for women readers with fashion news and advice columns.

Urban municipalities were providing landscaped public parks, sports fields and playgrounds, places to stroll or take the baby out. This may not have been quite what Wordsworth had in mind when he wrote of communing with wild nature, but as a visual and physical enhancement to the life of ordinary people it was no mean achievement.

Women everywhere were taking up golf.

Gas cookers were becoming popular as an alternative to solid fuel.

They were more compact and fitted into smaller kitchens.

In the USA Helen Keller, who had been blind, deaf and dumb from infancy, graduated from college with honours.

London car dealer Charles Rolls and Manchester engineer Henry Royce set up a partnership to manufacture luxury cars.

War broke out between Russia and Japan over disputed territories in Korea and Manchuria.

Dinner on deck (steerage class) – Mid-Atlantic – 1906

In the USA vast fortunes were being made from oil, steel, mining, railroads and bond dealing.

These millionaires were often ruthless in their treatment of immigrant workers, although some were generous, giving money to charities, medicine, art collections and universities.

Some wealthy families like the Vanderbilts married their daughters into the English aristocracy. The bride acquired a title and the grandeur of a country estate and a London mansion.

The bridegroom acquired the money to keep them up. Divorce was very rare – it was too expensive for the poor, and divorced women were disapproved of by middle-class society.

San Francisco, USA, was struck by a violent earthquake. Strong winds fanned the fires, flimsy wooden dwellings burned. There were huge casualties as people fled the city.

Hot-air ballooning was all the rage in Paris.

Norwegian explorer Roald Amundsen succeeded in opening up the Northwest Passage across northern Canada to the Pacific.

1906

Here is another family on the move, not for pleasure but out of desperate necessity. Cities were expanding all over the world, but none faster than in America, 'God's crucible, the Great Melting Pot', as Israel Zangwill, a Russian Jewish immigrant, called it. A barbarous massacre of Jews in his country the previous year, and other 'pogroms' like it, resulted in a flood of immigrants crossing the Atlantic to seek a better, safer life. With them came people from Ireland, Poland, Germany, the Balkans and numerous other countries – 9 million of them between 1900 and 1910. Very few spoke English. Many could not read or write in their own language.

The steerage fare across the Atlantic was as low as $10. Families embracing all age groups crowded below decks in packed and often squalid conditions. They disembarked at Ellis Island, where they underwent medical examinations and awaited official entry to the USA.

In the UK the campaign for votes for women was gathering pace, led by Mrs Emmeline Pankhurst and her daughter Christabel.

VOTES for WOMEN!

Liberal prime minister Campbell-Bannerman saw a deputation representing 500,000 suffragettes. He urged patience and a non-aggressive approach.

Finnish women were the first in Europe to get the vote.

The first Grand Prix motor race took place in Le Mans, France.

Feathers were a chic fashion item, especially from exotic birds like ospreys and ostrich.

In the USA social reformers like Florence Kelley were campaigning against child and female 'sweated' labour.

In Chicago immigrant workers had to pay bribes to get jobs in the meat-packing industry.

They worked in filthy conditions.

Men sometimes fell into vats of fat, which later went out labelled 'Durham's Pure Lard'.

Under pressure from the US Medical Association, the Pure Food and Drug Act was made law.

Jacob Riis and Lewis Hine, two crusading photographers, recorded the lives of newly arrived immigrants in the city slums of the USA.

Riis was the first photographer to use flash light, then a hazardous process.

The 'Gibson Girl', drawn by US magazine artist Charles Dana Gibson, personified female glamour.

Women's hair was long and worn elaborately pinned up.

As more and more branded products poured into the market, it paid to advertise.

On arrival in the big cities bewildered families tended to congregate near their fellow nationals in teeming tenements. Some received a helping hand, some faced exploitation from those already established. The bulk of Italian immigrants were men and boys, hoping to make enough money to send home. Some already settled immigrants acted as employment brokers, 'padrones', taking a cut from a newcomer's meagre wages. Working conditions were often appalling.

The persecution of Jews in Russia was aimed at all classes, so immigrants included professional, educated people. Many self-help organizations for Jews were formed.

Younger generation immigrants of every nationality were eager to embrace their new society, to cast off their European past and become true Americans. Older people clung to their old language and customs and the family meal was a daily ritual, a familiar ceremony in a strange land.

In the USA William Kellogg formed the Battle Creek Toasted Cornflake Company. Cornflakes were originally developed by his brother John to improve the diet of hospital patients.

In Britain *HMS Dreadnought*, the fastest and biggest battleship in the world, was launched.

Patriotic sailor suits were fashionable for boys and girls.

A census revealed that, with its colonies and protectorates, Britain now ruled about one fifth of the globe.

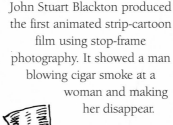

John Stuart Blackton produced the first animated strip-cartoon film using stop-frame photography. It showed a man blowing cigar smoke at a woman and making her disappear.

Scrubbing the doorstep spotlessly clean every morning was a matter of housewifely pride.

Cold leftovers – An English country estate – 1908

Gustav Mahler, conductor of the Vienna State Opera, composed his eighth symphony.

It was a sweeping orchestral work with mixed chorus, solo voices, boys' choirs and organ.

Suburban areas were being bought up for landscaped cemeteries.

People saved all their lives to make a last lavish show at their own funerals.

When a close relative died, adults and children wore black mourning clothes for many months.

There was a lot of work for dressmakers.

Kenneth Grahame's book *The Wind in the Willows* was first published. Its idyllic riverbank setting was, in reality, already being eaten away by development.

And a brisk trade in polished jet beads for mourning jewellery.

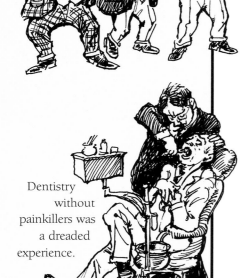

1908

W hen I was a schoolgirl in the 1930s we sang the happily now deleted version of the hymn 'All Things Bright and Beautiful' which went: 'The rich man in his castle, the poor man at his gate, God made them high and lowly and ordered their estate . . .'

In my picture two girls exchange looks across a cramped cottage kitchen. They are of similar age, but worlds apart. One has arrived with her mother, bringing charitable gifts of food to a family of poor tenants into which yet another baby has been born. This is part of their duty as the leisured, land-owning class. The other girl has probably worked ever since she can remember. Her schooling is scant: she has helped her mother with the endless chores, minded the younger children, fed the animals, worked in the vegetable patch and later in the fields. In her limited way she knows a good deal about life.

The classic hand or treadle Singer sewing machine (invented in the 19th century) had transformed dressmaking.

Many are still in use today.

Gaiters and 'spats' worn over boots or shoes were high fashion for men and women.

Dentistry without painkillers was a dreaded experience.

In Pittsburgh, USA, a new hardwearing floor-covering called Linoleum (Lino) was being marketed in bright colours to beautify the home.

It was very easy to clean.

Oil was first struck in Persia (now Iran) in the Middle East.

In the USA Henry Ford put his T-Model automobile on sale, priced $850.

He wanted to build a 'people's car' using an assembly-line method to speed up production.

It was a sturdy vehicle of light steel alloy.

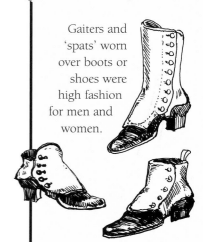

In Britain, nannies, often assisted by a nursemaid, ruled the nursery.

Splendid baby carriages were available for some lucky infants.

Country people often had to wash under a cold-water pump in the yard.

In the country people used wood for fuel as it was free.

Town dwellers burned coal, delivered to their door in sacks.

In Britain the chimney sweep, with his soot-blackened face, performed an essential domestic service. He pushed his circular brushes up chimneys using extended canes.

In Britain the Suffragette movement was becoming more forceful, assertive and defiant.

Imprisoned Suffragettes wore coarse, cotton clothes stamped with broad arrows.

Some went on hunger strike. They endured appalling conditions.

The first international football game was played in Vienna. England beat Austria 6–1.

Hockey, considered a very rough game, was being played by English schoolgirls.

At colleges all over Europe and America women were enjoying higher education.

But combining a career with matrimony was very unusual.

Medical schools were also opening their doors to women.

Country cottages might have appeared picturesque to visiting artists, but in reality many were damp, poorly ventilated and overcrowded. Ill health, particularly tuberculosis, was a scourge in the countryside as well as in the cities.

The upper-class girl in my picture has been far more protected. Her education, equally limited in its way, would be at home with a governess, concentrating on the social graces until it was time to 'come out', which meant attending balls and other social events in order to meet eligible young men.

None of these women, in common with most of their contemporaries in Europe and America, rich and poor, have a vote. Perhaps it has not yet occurred to many of them to want one. But radical changes in the lives of women were gathering momentum as never before in history. The looks on the faces of these two girls are on the one hand thoughtful and tentative, on the other defiant and perhaps scornful. But in their lifetimes barriers will come down in ways they never imagined.

The British Boy Scout movement, founded by Colonel Baden-Powell, was an immediate success.

The aims were teaching outdoor skills combined with a moral code, loyalty and self-reliance.

The Girl Guide movement soon followed.

French physicist Marie Curie's work resulted in her isolating pure radium for the first time in 1910. She won an unprecedented Second Nobel Prize in 1911.

At a conference in Switzerland the German physicist Albert Einstein put forward his quantum theory of light.

In Sydney, Australia, black US boxer Jack Johnson became world champion, beating Australian Tommy Burns after 14 rounds.

Johnson was hitting with such ferocity that the fight had to be stopped.

Economy menu – Boston, USA – 1910

This year Paris was affected by serious flooding. The elephants in the Jardin des Plantes suffered from rheumatism and a giraffe drowned.

Paris was the undisputed centre of European fashion and art.

Diaghilev's Russian Ballet had a huge impact on fashion and design.

Paris dress designers did away with corsets and produced narrow-skirted gowns of oriental richness.

Hat brims were getting even wider.

Tight 'hobble' skirts were hardly more liberating than corsets.

Violence stalked the streets of French cities in the form of young knife-carrying thugs called 'Apaches'.

1910

In my childhood we often sang songs around the piano to my mother's rather hit-and-miss accompaniment. One of my favourites was a ballad entitled 'One Meat Ball', the cautionary tale of a little man who forsook his wife's excellent cooking and 'walked up and down to seek a dinner in the town'. But, when inside the restaurant, he discovered to his acute embarrassment that the only item on the menu he could afford was 'one meat ball (without the gravy) . . .'

This song gave me the idea for my picture. But it was the sentimental Irish ballads like 'Molly Malone' and 'The Mountains of Mourne', so full of yearning and sadness, that really grabbed us. There was a large Irish population in Liverpool, near where we lived, who sang them with great feeling. Their parents may have been part of the great exodus from Ireland who never got further than Liverpool.

Realist novelists like British Arnold Bennett and H. G. Wells and American Theodore Dreiser were exploring the effects of rapid social change.

In Germany there was an atmosphere of nationalism.

Young officers and students prided themselves on their discipline and toughness.

Duelling with swords was a way of settling arguments.

Facial scars received in duels were a mark of valour and vanity.

American pianist and composer Scott Joplin's ragtime music had become enormously popular and influential.

Notorious British murderer Dr Crippen and his accomplice Ethel le Neve were arrested while escaping to Canada on the SS *Montrose,* thanks to ship-to-shore radio transmitters.

In the USA President Theodore Roosevelt was cracking down on police corruption.

Telephone exchanges were manual.

An operator took your number and plugged in the electrical connection.

The 'daffodil' telephone came into office and home use.

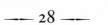

Most domestic laundry was done at home by hand or sent out to a washerwoman.

But help was at hand in Germany, where Carl Miele, inventor of industrial butter churns, began making washing machines.

Men and boys wore heavy socks and tweed suits with waistcoats in all seasons.

Dry cleaning and deodorants were not yet available.

Smaller items of laundry were scrubbed with soapsuds in the washtub.

Wool clothing was sponged over occasionally with ammonia.

Lightweight suits were a luxury item for the better-off man.

Larger items of laundry were boiled clean in a copper cauldron set over a brick fireplace.

Laundry bills could be reduced by wearing a 'wipe-clean' collar made of celluloid (an early type of plastic).

In 1910 Irish immigrants were pouring into the USA, fleeing from poverty and political unrest. The eastern seaboard cities such as Boston and New York teemed with crowded slums in which only the strongest prospered. The letters 'NINA' appended to job ads signified 'No Irish Need Apply'. But many of them did prosper, becoming, amongst other things, brewers, saloon keepers and restaurateurs, policemen and politicians.

Many bewildered, freshly arrived immigrants turned to their own countrymen for political representation. Some ambitious local politicians managed favours in exchange for votes and, inevitably, there was a good deal of City Hall corruption. Women, who had no vote, took what jobs they could. Work in restaurants and laundries was in some ways preferable to the garment sweatshops.

Wet laundry had to be wrung through a heavy hand-cranked iron mangle.

The US film industry was re-locating from New York to California. The sunny climate was more favourable to photography and labour was cheaper.

Mary Pickford was set to become one of the first idols of silent movies.

She became known as the World's Sweetheart.

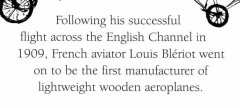

Following his successful flight across the English Channel in 1909, French aviator Louis Blériot went on to be the first manufacturer of lightweight wooden aeroplanes.

Electric irons had been invented but they weighed over 6 kilos.

Many women made do with 'flat irons', which they heated on the stove.

The British king Edward VII died and was succeeded by his son, George V.

He was more serious and less pleasure-loving than his father.

Supper on the sidewalk – St Louis, USA – 1912

Russian prima ballerina Anna Pavlova first danced her celebrated 'Dying Swan' at a royal command performance in London.

In the USA at least 2 million children were at work, doing monotonous and sometimes dangerous jobs.

Many of them were immigrants.

'The Elves' was the name for 15,000 or so 'Breaker Boys' under 16 who worked for the Pennsylvania Coal Company.

Their job was to pick slate out of coal from 7 a.m. to 5 p.m.

Immigrant workers found it hard to band together because they spoke so many different languages.

Vacuum cleaners, still cumbersome, were taking on a more recognizable form.

In Britain and Europe suburban domestic architecture tended to look back to a 'folksy' style, with mock beams and leaded windowpanes.

1912

In 1912 jazz music, rooted in the rhythms of an enslaved people, had already risen from the Mississippi delta 'like a Black Venus emerging from the foam', and was becoming popular and influential all over America. The mechanization of agriculture in the southern states had given rise to a steady flow of black workers leaving the land, first migrating to the cities of the South, then flocking in great numbers to the industrial cities of the North. I first discovered jazz in my late teens. Down at the youth club we usually danced to the highly orchestrated music of the 1940s big bands, led by Harry James, Artie Shaw and Glenn Miller. But it was on old 78 records that jazz performers like trumpet player Louis Armstrong, blues singer Bessie Smith and cornet player Bix Beiderbecke seemed to speak directly to me about surviving almost anything life could throw at you and emerging triumphantly with an amazing creative vitality.

There was a coalminers' strike in Britain. The men were attacked in the press as unpatriotic.

American newspaper cartoonist Winsor McCay was animating his famous 'Little Nemo' character.

But the full commercial potential of his idea had yet to be realized.

The National Association for the Advancement of Colored People had been founded in the USA, hoping to end racial discrimination.

W. E. B. Dubois was an important leader of the movement.

Norwegian explorer Roald Admundsen's expedition was the first to reach the South Pole. Captain Scott's British expedition arrived soon after, but all perished on their return journey. They were only a few miles from their food store. The Scott expedition used motorized sledges, which broke down, and horses, which died of cold.

The Norwegians used husky dogs to pull their sledges.

Huskies have thick coats and sweat through their noses, so can survive intense cold.

Belgian Adolf Sax's newly invented instrument the saxophone was heard in dance halls everywhere.

The Tango, a dance from Argentina, was the latest craze.

Pianist 'Jelly Roll' Morton, who claimed to be the father of jazz, was already recording in Chicago.

Young couples were scandalizing their elders with dances like the Bunny Hug and the Turkey Trot.

'Naturally regretted by all careful and clean-living people,' commented the *Girl's Own Paper*.

B etween 1910 and 1920 the combined black population of New York, Chicago, Philadelphia and Detroit had almost doubled. The new urban poor had their own dance halls, vaudeville theatres and bars, all of which required musicians. The commercial music industry, 'Tin Pan Alley', fuelled by the dance craze and advances in the recording industry, was quick to realize the popular potential of jazz.

But for black people the brief period of hope following the Civil War had given way to a long period of bitter despair, which did not lighten until the 1950s. In many states a wide range of segregationalist laws and other devices for taking away the black vote were rigorously applied. The infamous 'Jim Crow' laws (named after the clownish, blacked-up character in a minstrel show) controlled not only education and work but whole areas of civic life too.

Isadora Duncan's style of dance – barefoot natural movement inspired by that of ancient Greece – was attracting a huge following.

Mohandas Gandhi, a young Indian lawyer working in South Africa, became a founder member of a newly created civil rights group: the African National Congress.

Later, back in India, he led the campaign for Indian independence from Britain.

In Ireland over 400,000 Protestants signed a protest against the bill for home rule.

In Paris world-famous dancer Nijinsky gave an electrifying performance in the Russian Ballet's *Afternoon of a Fawn*, with music by Claude Debussy.

Leon Bakst designed the sets.

SS *Titanic*, the world's biggest and most luxurious liner, set sail from England to the USA. It struck an iceberg and sank in the icy North Atlantic.

It had been considered unsinkable. There were not enough lifeboats aboard.

Over 1,500 of its 2,224 passengers drowned.

Children's clothing was becoming lighter to allow more freedom of movement.

Tea in the garden – Surrey, England – Summer 1914

Women were needed to do jobs in munitions factories.

Compulsory conscription was not yet introduced but posters everywhere urged men to volunteer for the armed services.

Volunteer auxiliary nurses (VADs) faced up bravely to the grim and often menial tasks of military nursing.

1914

The summer of 1914 was warm and sunny all over Europe. People flocked to the seaside, went fishing, amused themselves at sports and fairgrounds or simply lazed in their back gardens. Few were aware of the political storm clouds which were growing over Europe. Britain, France and Russia were ranged in a series of complicated treaties against Germany, Austria and, later, Turkey.

Britain claimed to rule the waves. She had been enjoying a period of settled prosperity supported by the wealth of a great empire. Germany had been building her military might. Now the German ruler, Kaiser Wilhelm II, though first cousin of the British king, George V, was being portrayed in cartoons as a menacing bully. Another royal cousin, Tsar Nicholas II of Russia, a man who longed for a simple family life, rode at the head of an army which, in numbers at least, was the mightiest in the world.

George Bernard Shaw's play *Pygmalion* contained some bad language which shocked audiences.

Silent movie clown Charlie Chaplin, born in the London slums, was in Hollywood inventing one of the most famous film characters ever.

Cinemas were appearing everywhere. Audiences needed comedy to lighten the gloom.

The knockabout silent comedy films featuring the Keystone Kops were hugely popular.

New York socialite Mary Phelps Jacobs asked her maid to devise a bra out of two handkerchiefs and a ribbon.

This excellent idea was soon marketed.

Shorter, more practical skirts and tunic-style coats were reflecting the changing times.

Children delighted in toy howitzer guns which fired rubber shells.

Very soon real howitzers were to be put to a more deadly use on the Western Front.

Mexican rebel bandit Pancho Villa was being represented in the American press as a kind of Robin Hood.

A film company paid him $25,000 to allow them to film his battles.

He delayed a night attack to allow them to film by daylight.

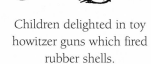

Prince Alexis, the boy heir to the Russian throne, suffered from an inherited blood disease, haemophilia, which was kept secret from the people.

He bled at the slightest injury and often had to be carried in public.

In spite of its huge numbers, the Russian cavalry was defeated on the Polish border by the well-organized modern German infantry.

Motor taxis were taking the place of horse-drawn cabs on the London streets.

The German emperor, nicknamed 'Kaiser Bill', was easy to caricature.

He wore a spiked helmet and an aggressively turned-up moustache.

Northern Ireland was on the brink of civil war over home rule.

The assassination by a Serb nationalist of Archduke Franz Ferdinand of Austria and his wife on a visit to Sarajevo in Bosnia was the flashpoint which plunged Europe into war.

Although this event was well before my time, it cast a long shadow over my parents' lives and those of many young adults like them. Patriotic fervour broke out everywhere. Young men hurried to enlist, urged by a widespread enthusiasm for war. A popular song of the time began: 'Oh, we don't want to lose you, but we think you ought to go . . .' and ended: 'We shall cheer you, thank you, kiss you when you come back again.'

By Christmas the opposing armies faced each other in France in lines of trenches and dugouts which stretched from the English Channel to the Swiss border – the Western Front. Four years later, after one of the most bitter conflicts in history, about 10 million servicemen never returned home. They had been killed in action in a war whose causes many of them hardly understood.

Cockney street traders still preferred donkey carts.

Horses and mules were still used by the army for transport at the front.

The Panama Canal, joining the North Atlantic and South Pacific Ocean, was completed.

The editor of the French newspaper *Le Figaro*, Monsieur Caillaux, attacked the finance minister Monsieur Calmette in print for being corrupt and pro German. Madame Calmette visited her hairdresser, had her nails done, then purchased a gun, drove to the *Figaro* office and shot Caillaux dead for insulting her husband.

A bill to give women the vote was rejected in France.

At Christmas, on a section of the Western Front, soldiers from opposing sides met and exchanged gifts.

Safety glass, developed for car windscreens, was also used for gas masks.

A mug of tea in a trench – Northern France – 1916

On Easter Monday Irish nationalists fighting for independence from Britain finally boiled over into full-scale rebellion.

In Ireland the Republican rebels seized the Dublin general post office and declared Ireland an independent republic.

British military reinforcements were brought in and the rebel leaders later executed.

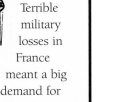

British women worked as farm labourers to help keep up food supplies.

Many foodstuffs were scarce but there was little official rationing.

Terrible military losses in France meant a big demand for mourning clothes.

Dresses could be dyed black in a day.

English poet and soldier Siegfried Sassoon's first war poems were patriotic, but his later work showed a bitter disillusion with life in the trenches. He was nicknamed 'Mad Jack' for his bravery, but his hatred of bloodshed led him to defy military authority.

Terrifying long-range shells could be fired from well behind the enemy lines into soldiers in their dugouts.

'Shell-shocked' was the description of men who suffered mental illness brought on by too much battle stress. They were sometimes wrongly accused of cowardice.

1916

I have always been drawn to public libraries as places of promise and romance, perhaps because my parents first met in Ramsgate public library in the dark days of the First World War. I like to think of them falling in love among the bookshelves. My dad was in the Royal Flying Corps stationed near there and, like so many other young servicemen, faced loneliness, fear and uncertainty, far from home. As shy people sometimes do at critical moments in their lives, he acted completely out of character and asked my mother if he could walk her home.

On the coast of Kent they could sometimes hear the big guns pounding away on the other side of the Channel. But many people at home had little real idea of the brutality of trench warfare. Newspaper reports remained determinedly upbeat, in spite of the daily notices they carried of those killed in action. News photography and newsreels, such as they were, had been heavily censored.

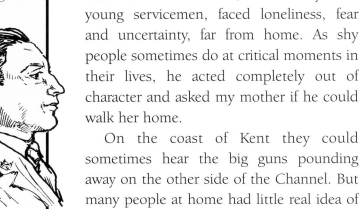

Better-off people could buy food and other luxuries on the 'black market'.

Men who made fortunes out of wartime shortages by selling on the black market were called 'profiteers'.

Master storyteller Rudyard Kipling lost his only son John, aged 18, early in the war and never fully recovered from the blow.

German submarines were inflicting terrible damage on transatlantic shipping.

The British liner SS *Lusitania* had been torpedoed and sunk in 1915.

US president Woodrow Wilson threatened to break off diplomatic relations with Germany if the submarine attacks continued.

In Russia corrupt monk and self-styled healer Grigori Rasputin had a magnetic hold over the tsarina, who was convinced he could cure her son of haemophilia. With the tsar away at war, Rasputin was thought to be influencing political decisions.

Aristocrats loyal to the tsar lured Rasputin to the house of Prince Yusupov, where he was poisoned and then shot dead.

They dumped his body in the river Neva.

British Nurse Edith Cavell, who had helped British soldiers escape, was shot by the Germans in 1915.

She had tended the wounded on both sides.

Rigid German airships called zeppelins bombarded London, but the theatres stayed open, playing to packed audiences.

Servicemen on leave were keen to enjoy the latest musical comedies such as *The Bing Boys* and *Chu Chin Chow.*

US car manufacturer Henry Ford doubled his workers' wages to create 'new consumers'. But he also speeded up the assembly line so that they had to work even harder.

A glamorous Dutch dancer called Mata Hari tried to act as a double agent, spying for both French and German officers.

She was arrested and shot by the French in 1917.

In the Battle of the Somme the British introduced a new weapon – the tank.

It could move over the roughest ground and withstand heavy artillery.

As the appalling losses at the front mounted and inexperienced replacement soldiers were recklessly thrown into battle, troops lost faith in their generals.

Officers were armed with revolvers, not rifles, so their outline was easy to pick off as they led their men 'over the top'.

The average life expectancy of a junior officer at the front was thought to be about six weeks.

Dashing fighter pilots like the German Baron von Richthofen (nicknamed the Red Baron) fought in the air above the battlefields. Military aircraft had now become an important part of warfare.

In France the long-drawn-out German assault on Verdun and the first Battle of the Somme resulted in pitiless slaughter. The USA, not yet involved in the war, was supporting the Allies financially, though President Wilson was under pressure at home to remain neutral.

French and British fought alongside soldiers from Canada, Australia, New Zealand and India against the Germans and their allies. They strafed and sniped at one another from the trenches by day, and at night went 'over the top' across barbed wire to face machine-gun fire. Small areas of No Man's Land were bitterly fought for, gained, lost and regained at enormous cost to life.

Troops in the trenches suffered the stench of death from bodies of comrades and foes alike, slept in cold, rat-infested dugouts and often moved about in heavy kit, knee-deep in mud. Fleas and body lice were a particular torment, as were the unbearable levels of noise. Patriotic songs like 'Pack Up Your Troubles' gave way to bitterness in the sarcastic 'Oh, What a Lovely War . . .'

In spite of the war the great French sculptor Auguste Rodin stayed in Paris. He died in 1917 aged 77.

The French artist Claude Monet, key figure of the Impressionist movement, was now old, with failing eyesight. But he was still painting magical, shimmering canvasses of water lilies in his garden at Giverny in northern France.

Homecoming tea – Yorkshire, England – 1918

On the Western Front a decisive battle at Amiens finally turned the tide against the German army.

Following the US declaration of war against Germany in 1917, American soldiers, nicknamed 'Doughboys', had arrived to fight at the front.

Engineers in Germany began work on an all-metal aeroplane.

A terrible flu epidemic swept through Europe, killing millions.

1918

The horrors of the First World War loomed over my childhood just as the shadow of the Holocaust and the US war in Vietnam has done over later generations. My own father survived, having never experienced the worst of it. Some of my schoolfriends had fathers who had returned without an arm or a leg; they struggled silently with mental illness brought on by their terrible memories. Reminders were everywhere. Every town and village had its war memorial and on Armistice Day, during the two minutes' silence, everything, including the traffic, stopped as people remembered the dead with bowed heads.

It was, they said, the 'war to end all wars', and politicians talked of building 'homes fit for heroes'. But many ex-servicemen who had survived found it hard to settle down, or to talk about what they had gone through, even to their families.

The war officially ended on 11 November, Armistice Day, which became a national holiday.

Peace at last! British crowds, delirious with relief, celebrated in the streets.

About 10 million had died, a greater loss than in any other single conflict.

The blood-red poppies which soon grew over the battlefields came to symbolize all those deaths.

War poet Wilfred Owen was killed in action a week before the war ended, aged 25.

One German soldier who survived the war was Corporal Adolf Hitler.

Peacetime saw the emergence of frivolous hats.

Many recruits had been found to be undernourished when they joined up.

In spite of bitter complaints about army food, the average soldier gained 10 kilos.

Some children found it hard to accept a father whom they hadn't lived with for years.

Revolution in Russia sent shock waves around the world.

It was feared that the workers in other countries would rebel under the Communist slogan: 'Workers of the world unite! You have nothing to lose but your chains!'

Tsar Nicholas II, who had already given up the throne and was under house arrest, was murdered with his wife and family by local revolutionaries.

Poster art in a distinctive graphic style played a big part in getting the Communist message across.

It was the first 'modern war'. At the beginning of the century the advance in science and technology was regarded as something that bestowed marvellous benefits and conveniences on mankind. Now its use in warfare showed it could also be sinister and menacing.

Great technological advances had been made in the power of explosives, the invention of tanks, the dreaded poison gas and, probably most importantly, in aviation and marine engineering. Alongside these were advances in medicine.

The old romantic image of a gallant cavalry officer charging into battle with his sword aloft was gone for ever. A hard-won supremacy at sea and America's entry into the war in 1917 finally turned the tide for the exhausted Allies. President Wilson outlined his peace proposals, including the removal of all trade barriers, complete freedom of navigation and the reduction of arms to the lowest point 'consistent with domestic safety'.

Following food riots in 1917 the demoralized Russian army revolted and sided with the people.

Vladimir Ilych Lenin, leader of the Communist Bolshevik Party, had returned from exile and was successfully leading the revolution.

Intellectual Leon Trotsky was a key figure behind events. All private property was to be taken into state control and land given to peasants.

Civil war broke out between the Bolsheviks (Reds) and the supporters of the tsar (Whites).

Recording onto discs was now the way to make dance bands famous.

Motorbikes, which had been a vital part of military messenger transport, now became vehicles for peacetime riding.

Passengers took their chances in the sidecar!

In the Syrian desert a young British officer known as Lawrence of Arabia led a successful Arab guerrilla revolt against the Turks.

Arabs were now liberated from the Ottoman (Turkish) Empire.

Lunch alone – Liverpool, England – 1920

Violent unrest in Ireland followed the British government's decision to split the country in two.

A bloody conflict developed, with atrocities on both sides.

Following the murders of British officers by the IRA (Irish Republican Army), a notoriously brutal British special force, the 'Black and Tans', fired on a Dublin football crowd.

Alcoholic liquor became illegal in the USA. This was called 'Prohibition'.

The Russian civil war ended in victory for the Communist Red Army, led by Leon Trotsky.

But the Russian economy was in disastrous trouble.

American architect Frank Lloyd Wright was pioneering a unique approach to building design.

1920

High hopes were pinned on the newly formed League of Nations, based in Geneva, Switzerland. The defeated German army had trickled homewards, but many British and French soldiers were still stationed in the occupied zones of Germany. Old enemies mixed together in pubs; men who had been trying to kill each other a short time before swapped experiences in a bond of soldiering, while politicians argued the harsh terms of peace.

The long fight for votes for women in Britain and the USA was won at last. Women had proved themselves in wartime by doing hard, responsible jobs while the men were away fighting. British women over thirty had won the vote in 1918. In the US, where support had to be fought for in every state, they finally reached their goal. The era of the 'career woman' had begun in earnest. But there also emerged another type, the young, carefree 'flapper', hell-bent on having a good time, smoking in public and totally unconcerned about world affairs.

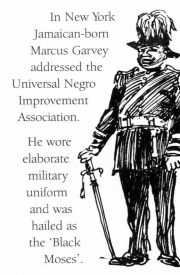

In New York Jamaican-born Marcus Garvey addressed the Universal Negro Improvement Association.

He wore elaborate military uniform and was hailed as the 'Black Moses'.

Cafés and teashops began to cater for ladies eating together or alone.

In the USA French artist Marcel Duchamp exhibited a urinal as a work of art.

The peace of the countryside was being shattered by motor-coach tours.

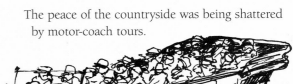

Post-war 'Bohemian' café life thrived on outrageous new ideas in art and literature.

A modernist art movement called 'Dada' set out to shock the established art world.

Short hair and shorter skirts were coming into style for young women, along with more liberated behaviour.

Many homes now had comfortable indoor bathrooms, with hot water supplied by a gas-fuelled 'geyser'.

Female secretaries were expected to master shorthand and the modern typewriter. They also had to know how to please their boss . . .

who was almost always a man.

The New York Yankees baseball team signed up 24-year-old 'Babe' Ruth, a left-handed pitcher, for a record-breaking $125,000.

American tycoons like Henry Ford and Harvey Firestone were getting back to nature by camping in the backwoods.

But they did it in luxury, with spacious tents, comfortable beds and electric light.

A common sight in the streets of Liverpool, where my newly married parents had set up home, was a group of ex-servicemen shuffling along in the gutter playing their old marching songs on makeshift instruments in the hope of collecting a few coppers. They were still around in my childhood. We always gave them money.

The war had given a huge boost to industry, and large fortunes had been made in armaments manufacture. But this prosperity and the employment that came with it dwindled in peacetime. Many homecoming servicemen found neither work nor a place to live at an affordable rent easy to come by. British prime minister Lloyd George launched plans to build houses and flats with government money.

Modernization was in the air. In Germany the architect Walter Gropius had founded his school of art and architecture, teaching a functional style suitable for an industrial age.

In the USA skyscrapers, symbols of America's growing power and wealth, were being built higher and higher.

It was known as 'the land grab in the sky'.

In 1919 British scientist Ernest Rutherford was the first to split the smallest known particle of the atom.

This had a devastating impact on the 20th century which few then dreamed of.

In Germany a newly formed extremist party, the National Socialists (Nazis), adopted a swastika as its symbol.

Sunday lunch – A Scottish suburb – 1922

The British Broadcasting Company (BBC) began making radio broadcasts.

The aim was to provide a high standard of talks, news, music and popular entertainment – to educate as well as amuse a wide public.

Bold patterns, influenced by modern art, were used by Paris dress designers like Doucet, Lelong and Coco Chanel, who made the cardigan fashionable.

Radio audiences at home used earphones for 'listening in'.

These inspired a fashionable hairstyle of plaits coiled over the ears.

But many young women preferred to have their hair 'bobbed'.

They wore powder, rouge and lipstick to emphasize their 'cupid's bow' lips, inspired by movie stars.

1922

Throughout my schooldays I cannot recall being taught by a man. All our teachers were unmarried women, most of whom we regarded as rather dreary. But now I realize that they were struggling to make a life for themselves on a low income, often supporting an elderly parent. The devastating losses of the war had resulted in a chronic shortage of men of marriageable age.

Working-class women, though poorly paid, always had a sturdy independence. But for a middle-class woman without higher education the options were limited. Work in a factory or as a domestic servant was unthinkable. Some managed to qualify to become teachers or secretaries. Some worked from home, dressmaking or giving music lessons, or took on the rather uncertain role of live-in governess or 'lady companion'.

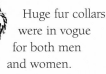

Huge fur collars were in vogue for both men and women.

In the USA illegal drinking clubs called 'speakeasies' were opening everywhere.

French tennis star Suzanne Lenglen popularized the wide headband and loose pleated tennis skirt.

British school girls wore pleated 'gym slips' over a white blouse with a tie.

Profits from the outlawed trade in 'bootleg' alcohol were enormous. Rival gangs were highly organized and there were violent clashes between them.

Benito Mussolini, leader of the Italian Fascist Party, marched on Rome with 30,000 'blackshirt' supporters. The Italian king, Victor Emmanuel, fearing civil war, made him prime minister. He was set to take absolute power.

Bram Stoker's novel *Dracula* was made into a film, *Nosferatu*, by avant garde director Friedrich Murnau. He used strange camera angles to terrifying effect.

There was destitution in Germany when the value of the Deutschmark went into freefall.

Times were hard after the war, even for the victorious nations. The map of Europe had changed drastically under the post-war treaties. Germany was particularly weakened and life there was grim.

It was said that the seeds of the European dictatorships to come were sown in the treaties that followed the First World War. President Wilson wanted a settlement which would give the new Europe a chance to recover. But Britain and France were in a vengeful mood. They wanted the Germans to pay dearly for their aggression and harsh terms of compensation were imposed on them.

In the USA the 1920 law forbidding the consumption of alcohol in all states had only succeeded in driving drinking underground. Illegal drinking clubs were opened, alcohol being illicitly produced and distributed by armed gangs. The heyday of the American gangster had arrived!

Experimental Irish writer James Joyce published *Ulysses*, a gigantic novel set in his native Dublin.

Many readers found it difficult to understand.

Novelists Virginia Woolf and D. H. Lawrence were reflecting English life from two very different viewpoints.

In Russia there had been a terrible famine, with 18 million people starving amid outbreaks of typhus and cholera.

Lenin's Communist policies were facing much criticism.

American newspaper comic strips, full of lively invention, were mostly aimed at adults. They were considered rather vulgar.

But now the British press began to run comic strips for children.

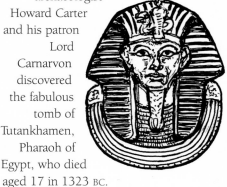

In a remote Egyptian valley, archaeologist Howard Carter and his patron Lord Carnarvon discovered the fabulous tomb of Tutankhamen, Pharaoh of Egypt, who died aged 17 in 1323 BC.

There was a treasure house of wonderful gold and jewelled artefacts and the pharaoh's coffin. The coffin was not opened until 1924, revealing the mummy covered by a solid gold bejewelled mask.

On one of the walls a curse was uncovered predicting the death of anyone who disturbed the tomb.

Lord Carnarvon died of a blood infection four months after the discovery.

Much-loved characters like Mary Tourtel and Alfred Bestall's 'Rupert Bear' and A. B. Payne's 'Pip, Squeak and Wilfred' began to appear.

Their success was followed up with fan clubs and hardcover Christmas annuals.

Coffee – Paris, France – 1924

Winter sports had become a huge tourist attraction in France and Switzerland.

Silent movie idols like Rudolph Valentino and Clara Bow were adored by audiences worldwide.

Another big movie star was a German shepherd dog called Rin Tin Tin.

He had been found as a puppy in a trench during the First World War by Lieutenant Lee Duncan, who had trained him to do amazing stunts.

The first Winter Olympics were held at Chamonix in the French Alps.

The only event open to women was figure skating.

British mountaineer George Mallory died in an attempt to climb Mount Everest.

German Nazi leader Adolf Hitler was imprisoned for an attempt to seize power.

The previous year he had burst into a Munich beer hall with his supporters, declaring, 'A national revolution has begun!'

1924

From as far back as I can remember I always wanted to be some kind of artist or designer, although I had no idea how to achieve this. When I was young it was Paris rather than Rome or New York which ruled supreme as the centre of not only fashion but all the arts, a position it had held since the beginning of the century.

In the 1920s this was at its height, when modernism inspired artists, novelists, poets and musicians to rub shoulders and exchange ideas at studio parties and cafés in the Latin Quarter. American novelists like F. Scott Fitzgerald and Ernest Hemingway lived there, as did Irish writer James Joyce and painters Braque and Picasso. There was a colony of Russian aristocrats and intellectuals, now impoverished refugees from the revolution. Black American performers like jazz clarinettist Sydney Bechet and dancer Josephine Baker worked there to escape the colour prejudice in their own country.

Women in non-Catholic countries were using birth control to limit the size of their families to one or two children.

Bottle feeding babies became widely accepted. Mothers were advised to follow a strict four-hourly timetable.

For the first time the flat-chested, narrow-hipped boyish figure was in fashion.

In affluent countries words like 'slimming' and 'dieting' entered the vocabulary.

In Russia (now called the Soviet Union) the leader Lenin died, leaving a serious power gap. Army chief Leon Trotsky and Joseph Stalin, General Secretary of the Communist Party, were the main possible successors.

Indian nationalist leader Mohandas Gandhi went on hunger strike as a protest against the violence between Muslims and Hindus.

British author E. M. Forster's last novel, *A Passage to India*, was set against a background of Anglo-Indian tensions.

'Cloche' hats were worn pulled down over the brow.

Women aviators like American Amelia Earhart inspired helmet-like hats with earflaps.

The French beret, traditionally a working man's headgear, became high fashion for both men and women.

Luxury hotels opened in resorts all along the coast of southern France and northern Italy.

The 'new rich', like munitions manufacturers and profiteers who had made fortunes from the war, could afford high prices!

Advertisements for smoking were now aimed at women as well as men.

Long cigarette-holders were an elegant fashion accessory.

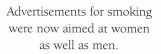

Now that more and more workers laboured indoors in factories and offices a suntan became a sign of affluent leisure.

The Vortex by young British playwright Noël Coward was performed in London.

The glamorous way to cross the Atlantic was on a luxury liner like the *Mauritania* or the *Normandie* – floating palaces with lavish state rooms, dining rooms and lounges for the wealthy traveller. On the promenade decks there were constant diversions, deck games and swimming pools. Rival shipping companies like Cunard and White Star competed to build bigger and faster ships to attract customers.

The French and Italian Riviera had from the beginning of the century been an attraction for smart tourists, who wanted to be seen on the esplanade at Nice or Menton or to gamble at Monte Carlo. Air travel across the English Channel, though growing fast, was still in its infancy. Most tourists took the boat train, which offered those who could afford it comfortable overnight sleepers and restaurant cars. For the even more adventurous there was the glamorous Orient Express and other services which crossed Europe to Istanbul.

Poster design played a big part in selling the glamour of travel.

American composer George Gershwin's *Rhapsody in Blue*, with its electrifying clarinet opening, was acclaimed in New York.

The Charleston was the latest dance craze.

The possibility of a shipboard romance was part of the attraction of transatlantic travel. Seasickness was one of the features not advertised.

Dancer Josephine Baker introduced it to Paris.

It was announced in the British Parliament that plans for a Channel tunnel were to be scrapped.

The first UK airline, Imperial Airways, took off with a fleet of 13 aeroplanes.

In the USA gangsters were moving into all areas of crime. In Chicago Al Capone became boss of the 'crime syndicate' of the city. Shopkeepers and restaurateurs were forced to pay 'protection' money to the mobs to avoid having their businesses smashed up, or worse. A corrupt mayor and police force made it easy for the gangs to operate.

A picnic by the sea – England – 1926

Late breakfast – London – 1928

In the UK the right to vote was given to all women over 21. It was called the 'Flapper Vote'.

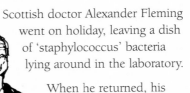

Scottish doctor Alexander Fleming went on holiday, leaving a dish of 'staphylococcus' bacteria lying around in the laboratory.

When he returned, his observations of the accumulated mould started him on research which ended in the discovery of penicillin.

The cinema had been revolutionized by the addition of sound when, in 1927, Al Jolson talked and sang in *The Jazz Singer*.

Exaggerated styles of acting began to look dated. Some silent movie stars like Douglas Fairbanks did not survive long in the 'talkies'. Another skill which went out with the arrival of sound was that of the cinema pianist.

Handsome American aviator Charles Lindbergh was being hailed as a hero for making the first solo flight across the Atlantic in 1927. His single engine monoplane was called the *Spirit of St Louis*.

In Russia Soviet leader Joseph Stalin was consolidating his power by removing the opposition. Leon Trotsky had been expelled from the Communist Party in 1927.

1928

In the romantic movies of my youth the glamorous star was often attended by a lady's maid. It was not much of a part, but I often wondered about this character. Few of the authors I read then, with the exception of Frances Hodgson Burnett and Arnold Bennett, explored the plot through a servant's eyes. (Only later did I discover that this was one of the great themes of drama and literature.)

My mother employed two servants – 'the maids'; they were called Jenny and Nellie. This was considered fairly modest by the middle-class standards of the time. They were as important and influential to my sisters and me as childminders are to the families of today's working mothers. We spent a lot of time mooching around in the kitchen, licking spoons of icing sugar and listening to the fascinating snatches of gossip, some of which was not intended for our ears. Though we knew all about Jenny and Nellie's relatives, we never met them. The social barrier was absolute.

They improvised throughout the film, adapting the mood of the music to the action on the screen.

British footballer Dixie Dean achieved a record 60 goals in his 1927–8 season with Everton, when he scored a hat trick against Arsenal.

Popular cartoon character Felix the Cat, created by Australian cartoonist Pat Sullivan, now had a serious rival, Mickey Mouse.

Mickey was the joint creation of American animators Walt Disney and Ub Iwerks.

In *Steamboat Willie* Walt Disney gave Mickey a voice (his own).

American Louis Armstrong (Satchmo), the greatest jazz trumpet improviser ever, made his classic recording of 'Basin Street Blues'.

It was a celebration of his birthplace, New Orleans.

'Camiknickers', a new item of female underwear, had appeared.

They were formed by joining a 'camisole' top to knickers to create a single garment.

Electric washing machines had hand-driven mangles attached.

Art Deco was an inspiration for set designers of Hollywood musicals.

New York skyscrapers, like the Art Deco Chrysler building with its metal-clad spire, were dubbed 'Cathedrals of Commerce'.

The 'beehive' fridge had the cooling machinery on top to make more room inside.

'Servants', announced an article in *Good Housekeeping* in the early 1920s, 'are as rare as blackberries in May.' There does seem to have been a shortage of domestic labour, in spite of the excess of females in the population. Perhaps young women preferred work in a shop or factory to the restrictions imposed by a 'live-in' job.

An ever more glittering array of labour-saving devices was becoming available, offering housewives a magic freedom from drudgery. Interior design flowered into the Art Deco style. Influenced by streamlined architecture and modern art, furniture and domestic appliances favoured squared-off cubist shapes, zigzags, swooping curves and highly stylized geometric decoration. It was a style which represented a cosmopolitan glamour. At first it was bought only by the wealthy, but soon, with mass production and the relative cheapness of synthetic materials, a little bit of Hollywood glitz was available to all.

Even the maid's uniform had a smart Art Deco look.

Elegant furniture was made in two contrasting tones of wood, as in Abel Faidy's dining table.

Domestic objects of all kinds were being given a desirably stylish look.

Ceramic designers Clarice Cliff and Susie Cooper used clean-cut shapes and bold patterns.

Civil war in China ended when nationalist general Chiang Kai-shek's army entered Peking. China was now unified under his rule.

Le Corbusier's armchair was in black leather and chrome.

In the USA ruthless gangsters were now armed with sub-machine-guns and drove around in bullet-proof Cadillacs.

J. Edgar Hoover, now director of the Federal Bureau of Investigation, was waging war against bootleggers.

The new movie comedy duo, skinny, 'dim-witted' Stan Laurel (British) and fat, bossy Oliver Hardy (American), made their hilarious debut.

Betty Joel's desk was all streamlined curves with no angles.

Soup – Pittsburgh, USA – 1930

Soviet leader Joseph Stalin set out to 'modernize' Russian agriculture by declaring all farmland collectively owned.

Peasants were now forced to work on vast state-owned farms for a wage instead of cultivating their own land.

In the USA factories closed, throwing millions out of work.

The flow of people into the big cities was reversed as many began roaming the country in search of work.

Thousands of ruthless special agents were sent to enforce the scheme.

In much of Britain and Europe country dwellers stuck to the old ways in spite of modernization.

Horses still played a big part in rural life.

Farm labourers drove their carts through water now and then to swell the wood and tighten the wheels.

Routine work like hoeing turnips was still done manually.

1930

The roof fell in on a pleasure-seeking decade when, in 1929, the New York stock exchange collapsed. During the post-war boom millions of people had invested for a quick profit. But when the US economy slowed down, some stocks were found to be overpriced and there was panic selling. Banks called in loans. The stock exchange went into free fall. Fortunes were wiped out overnight. By 1930 a full-scale depression had set in, with repercussions all over the world.

In the USA millions of unemployed stood in long lines in the desperate hope of a few days' casual work. Many became drifters, hobos hopping free rides on freight trains, sleeping rough. Squalid shanty towns appeared on the edges of cities, frail makeshift dwellings occupied by destitute families. They were named 'Hoovervilles' after the US president, who appeared powerless to help them. A bitter hit song of the era was 'Brother, Can You Spare a Dime?'

Worst hit by the Wall Street Crash were small investors.

Angry crowds besieged banks which had failed, taking all their savings.

There were big-time losers too. The Vanderbilt family lost $40 million in railroad stock alone and the Rockefellers lost four fifths of their fortune.

But they were not made homeless as so many Americans were.

Rubber boots made a big difference to the comfort of rural workers.

In Britain families of poor Londoners regularly went to Kent to help with the hop picking. It was their annual holiday!

The first World Cup football match was played in Montevideo, South America. Uruguay beat Argentina 4–2.

Australian cricketer Donald Bradman scored a record 452 runs in Sydney.

British aviator Amy Johnson left Britain, almost unnoticed, to make a solo flight to Australia in her *Gypsy Moth* aircraft.

She arrived 19 days later to international acclaim, having made one forced landing in Java.

Indian spiritual and political leader 'Mahatma' Gandhi led a 380-km march across India to the sea in protest against the tax on salt imposed by British rule.

Skirts, having reached their shortest ever, were now getting longer via the uneven hemline.

The 'Eton crop' was the latest extreme of short hair for women before hairstyles too began to get longer.

Glamorous, husky-voiced Swedish movie star Greta Garbo triumphantly survived the arrival of talking pictures.

Her first words on screen were, 'Gif me a visky and don't be stingy, baby!'

Although I was only an infant at this time, I grew up in the shadow of the Depression which hit Liverpool very hard, with its dependency on the Lancashire textile industry (cotton mostly). The 'dole' (unemployment benefit) was very minimal then. In an impoverished area of south Wales, one of my aunts and her clergyman husband worked unceasingly for the families of unemployed miners on an income not much higher than those of their parishioners.

Pawnshops, where hard-pressed people pledged their household belongings, even their overcoats, for a few shillings in the forlorn hope of redeeming them at the end of the week, thrived. The Salvation Army offered, as always, positive help in the form of food and clothing as well as the hope of salvation in heaven! The cinema, especially now that the 'talkies' had arrived, also thrived, offering a brief escape into musicals, westerns, swash-buckling adventure and romance.

Many young people working in big cities felt isolated and lonely. This mood was reflected in contemporary fiction as well as the paintings of American artist Edward Hopper.

A new planet was discovered in our solar system by astronomer Clyde Tombaugh. It was named Pluto after the Greek god of the underworld.

In North Africa Ras (Duke) Tafari was crowned 'King of the kings'. He became Emperor Haile Selassie of Abyssinia (now Ethiopia).

Acrylic plastics (Perspex) were invented.

The BBC had begun broadcasting daily television programmes but very few people owned sets on which to watch them.

Passenger airships were an exciting development in civil aviation.

In 1929 British crowds had seen the world's biggest airship, the *R101*, circle over London.

Also in 1929 Dr Hugo Eckner had piloted his giant German-built *Graf Zeppelin* on a flight around the world.

In Britain it was estimated that 2 million children were living in unfit housing. A programme of slum clearance began.

A business lunch – Hamburg, Germany – 1932

Hitler's Nazi Party made a special appeal to the young unemployed.

Dr Antonio de Oliviera Salazar became dictator of Portugal, introducing a new authoritarian state.

In Italy Benito Mussolini's Fascist government had complete power.

Only Fascist-sympathizing newspapers were allowed.

In Britain Sir Oswald Moseley, an admirer of Mussolini, founded the British Union of Fascists.

They were named the 'Blackshirts' and stirred up hatred against Jews in London's East End.

American musician Adolph Rickenbacker introduced his electric guitar.

Few people realized what a revolutionary effect this would have on popular music.

Radio sets were being constantly remodelled.

In Britain there were riots against the hated 'means test', which required the unemployed to reveal the income of the entire family. If their 'means' were considered adequate their dole was stopped.

1932

My 1932 picture is hardly a relaxed occasion. It is, I hope, fairly easy to spot the luckless businessman whose firm is going under. I have set it in Hamburg but it could just as easily be any industrial city in Europe or the USA at this time. There were plenty of predators circling, ready to take over bankrupt businesses.

It has been said that when America catches a cold, Europe sneezes. And as at any time of uncertainty and unemployment, people cast around for scapegoats, blaming incompetent government and 'foreigners'. This was especially so in Germany, where the deepening Depression and disenchantment with their leadership led to increasing support for Adolf Hitler's extreme right-wing National Socialist (Nazi) Party.

In the US presidential election, however, the Democratic candidate Franklin D. Roosevelt won a landslide victory over President Hoover, offering an optimistic 'New Deal' programme of reforms in the coming years.

Car design was becoming more streamlined, like the Bentley 3½ litre, which became available in 1933.

'Happy Days Are Here Again!' was the US Democratic Party's theme song, ushering in Franklin D. Roosevelt's presidency.

He had been stricken by polio, leaving his legs paralysed. He was unable to stand without heavy leg braces or walk unassisted.

He was an enormously energetic politician with great popular appeal.

The BBC moved into its new London headquarters in Portland Place.

It was a splendid modern building, curved like a liner, with towering radio masts.

The tragic monster from Mary Shelley's novel *Frankenstein* was acted by Boris Karloff in James Whale's 1931 Hollywood movie.

British novelist Aldous Huxley's *Brave New World*, a chilling vision of a scientific Utopia gone terribly wrong, was first published.

Zip fasteners, used by the US army in the First World War, were now rust proof and used in all kinds of clothing and luggage.

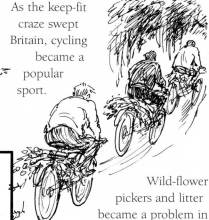
In musical comedies at the theatre high-kicking showgirls often compensated for a flimsy plot.

Cinemas like Henri Belloc's Gaumont Palace in Paris typified Art Deco glamour.

As the keep-fit craze swept Britain, cycling became a popular sport.

Wild-flower pickers and litter became a problem in rural beauty spots.

German physicist Albert Einstein dated the age of the planet Earth at 10 billion years.

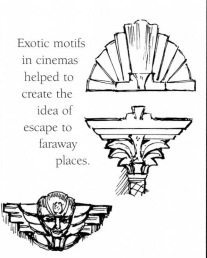
Exotic motifs in cinemas helped to create the idea of escape to faraway places.

Cinema usherettes and doormen wore smart uniforms.

Groceries were delivered to the door by errand boys on bicycles.

I n our quiet suburban seaside town, the news came to us from newspapers and the radio. Without the graphic realities of television, world events seemed fairly remote. We were aware that some families who had been well-to-do were now very hard up, and grinding poverty was sadly all too present on the streets of Liverpool. But some businesses, including my father's store, managed to thrive in spite of the Depression.

The entertainment business was one of these. Small cinemas now co-existed alongside the plush Picture Palaces, with their elaborate Art Deco architecture, restaurants, carpeted foyers and sweeping staircases. They offered a double bill of two feature films as well as 'shorts' and newsreels. In the interval a giant Wurlitzer organ rose like magic out of the floor in a blaze of coloured lights, and a dinner-jacketed organist gave a recital of hit tunes. Theatres thrived too, especially with light drawing-room comedies and variety shows with acrobats, comedians and chorus girls.

The Sydney Harbour bridge opened in Australia after nine years in construction.

In the U.S.A. Mexican artist Diego Ribera was at work on his *Detroit Industry Murals*, commissioned by the Ford Motor Company.

In the USA fast-food drive-ins were all the rage. Many were stylishly eye-catching.

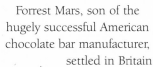
Forrest Mars, son of the hugely successful American chocolate bar manufacturer, settled in Britain and began to conquer the UK chocolate market.

Skirts were longer, cut on the cross and smoothly slim over the hips.

Beach pyjamas were high fashion.

So were floating chiffon dresses.

Dawn breakfast – A coffee stall, London – 1934

Stylish, functional furniture in tubular steel with leather upholstery typified 1930s chic, but it required a lot of space!

In Germany Hitler set about consolidating his power. In Hitler Youth organizations children were taught that their first loyalty was to him and Nazism, not to their families.

With increasing traffic, road safety was becoming a concern in Britain. Transport minister Leslie Hore-Belisha introduced driving tests, as well as pedestrian crossings and the flashing orange lights which the public named 'Belisha beacons' in his honour.

Cat's-eye road studs, invented by Percy Shaw, were introduced.

Jascha Heifetz, probably the most gifted and technically accomplished violinist of the century, recorded works by Elgar, Richard Strauss and Claude Debussy.

It was a sad loss to music when three leading British composers died: Sir Edward Elgar, Frederick Delius and Gustav Holst.

German scientist Dr Rudolph Kühnhold carried out the first practical radar tests.

Japan now controlled Manchuria in north-east China, where Pu Yi, once the boy emperor of China, was installed as a puppet ruler.

1934

In Britain, as in Europe and America, it was heavy industry, like steel production, mining and shipbuilding, that was worst hit by the Depression. Well-off people living in the more affluent areas of the country seemed hardly aware of the hardship, malnutrition and hopelessness being endured by the unemployed.

For those who did have a little money to spend, stylish, inexpensive off-the-peg clothes were now available. The jazzy styles of the 1920s were giving way to sleeker elegance, heavily influenced by the cinema. Screen goddesses like Marlene Dietrich and Katherine Hepburn, with their heavy-lidded, high-cheekboned faces which lent themselves so well to dramatically lit movie close-ups, were models of sophistication, as were their suave, pencil-moustached leading men.

German housewives were being encouraged to combine housework with graceful, body-toning gymnastics.

French artist Henri Matisse cut up paper shapes to design his simplified mural of dancing figures.

Superbly anarchic Hollywood comics the Marx Brothers were delighting audiences with movies like *Horse Feathers* and *Duck Soup*.

Groucho was the master wisecracker, Harpo was a mime and Chico played a gullible, zany Italian American.

Hollywood movie monster, the giant gorilla King Kong, had made its terrifying appearance in 1933.

Excitement about the prehistoric monster believed to be lurking in Scottish Loch Ness increased when a photograph was published taken by someone who claimed to have spotted it.

UK tennis star Fred Perry won the men's singles championships at Wimbledon.

Beaming Italian dictator Mussolini was among the spectators when his team won the World Cup against Czechoslovakia 2–1.

In the USA President Roosevelt's first 'hundred days' introduced a sweeping range of 'New Deal' policies to deal with the Depression.

The Hoover dam at Lake Mead was one of the more ambitious 'New Deal' undertakings.

Another was to supply cheap electric power to people relying on primitive motor generators and kerosene lamps.

President Roosevelt explained his 'New Deal' policies to the American people on the radio in a series of friendly 'fireside chats'.

When Prohibition ended the shady world of illegal 'speakeasies' disappeared and sales of alcohol rocketed.

Alcoholic cocktails featuring exotic mixtures were now fashionable. Cocktail bars opened everywhere.

Sophisticated names like 'Manhattan' and 'Highball' were used to make cocktail drinking popular on both sides of the Atlantic.

Skirts were long and slinky and often cut on the cross.

Pillbox hats with eye veils were fashionable; so were fox furs, complete with head, paws and tail!

Marlene Dietrich demonstrated the glamour of plucked eyebrows and wearing men's clothes.

In the USA President Roosevelt's 'New Deal' policy, designed to end the Depression, alleviate suffering and get people back to work, was beginning to take effect.

It included relief for the unemployed and work on government-funded projects – building roads, bridges, railroads, hydro electric dams, schools and libraries.

However, events in Europe were increasingly menacing. In Germany Hitler's Nazi Party had taken advantage of the weak government and disastrous economy. When in 1933 the Reichstag (parliament building) was burned down Hitler blamed it on a Communist plot. He managed to seize power. Like Mussolini he achieved it by almost legal means, and then proceeded to destroy democracy.

In the USSR Stalin was forcibly imposing his will. He wanted a strong, self-sufficient country and was prepared to destroy millions of his own people to achieve his aims. In 1933, and in future purges, he ruthlessly removed all political opposition.

J. Edgar Hoover, who controlled the Federal Bureau of Investigation, was not only tough on crime; he gathered intelligence on US citizens he considered 'subversive', such as trades union leaders, Communists and black civil rights workers.

Hollywood had promised not to make violent movies – except those showing heroic G-men (of the FBI) fighting crime.

President Roosevelt's wife Eleanor was very influential. She was his ears and eyes, giving his presidency a human touch. She toured the country, visiting schools, asylums, prisons and hospitals, talked to poor people everywhere and campaigned tirelessly against colour discrimination.

Nursery tea – Kensington, London – 1936

In the shipbuilding area of Jarrow in northern England unemployment had reached 80%.

To the accompaniment of mouth organs, Jarrow men marched to London in protest. Many cheered them on their way but the government remained unmoved.

A bloody civil war had broken out in Spain. The rebel nationalist army was led by the ruthless General Franco. They were much better armed than the republicans as they received support from Germany and Italy. The republicans received help from the USSR and from volunteers of the International Brigade, which included many Americans and British, such as novelist George Orwell.

At smart British children's parties the boys wore formal suits with waistcoats, striped trousers and 'Eton' collars.

Children attended classes to learn formal ballroom dancing and etiquette.

The little princesses, daughters of the British Duke and Duchess of York, were models of childhood elegance and decorum.

1936

As many parts of the world struggled with the Depression, civil war and invasion, British upper-class life remained relatively unchanged. In wealthy homes Nanny still reigned supreme. She and her charges lived in a separate area of the household, leaving parents free to entertain their friends, go out and lead their own lives. Nanny supervised a regime of plain food, fresh air and plenty of exercise. She was expected to teach the children good manners, keep them quiet, and produce them, clean and tidy, in the drawing room, where their parents played with them for an hour or two after tea.

Nannies were usually unmarried women, some of whom stayed with the family for many years, lavishing affection on their charges. Others were not so warm hearted. When little boys reached the age of seven or so they were routinely taken out of this highly protected environment and plunged into the rigours of an all-male boarding school.

US writer Ernest Hemingway went there as a war reporter.

In 1935, under the pretext of extending the Italian empire, Mussolini launched an attack on defenceless Abyssinia (now Ethiopia).

'I adore war,' Mussolini declared. 'War is to a man what childbirth is to a woman.'

In Germany Hitler had decreed that all Jews be deprived of their citizenship and barred from many professions.

Princess Elizabeth was soon to be in direct line to the throne when first her grandfather George V died and then her uncle, Edward VIII, abdicated before his coronation.

This was because he wanted to marry a twice-divorced American, Wallis Simpson, who could not be accepted as queen.

His brother, the Duke of York, became the new king, George VI. He was a family man, shy and suffering from a stammer which he bravely tried to overcome.

The newly designed Volkswagen – the 'people's car' – would, Hitler hoped, do for Germany what the Ford had done for the USA.

In Germany jobs were created building excellent roads, Autobahns, intended for troop movement as well as civilian traffic.

Marriages between Jew and non-Jew were illegal.

Hitler's army marched unopposed into the Rhineland, an area which had been lost by Germany to France after the First World War.

In the USA gigantic clouds of dust continued to sweep across the plains of the Midwest, destroying crops, dwellings and huge acres of farmland. One Kansas woman described them as 'the ultimate darkness'.

Thousands of farming families were left destitute. They took to the road in old cars and trucks or fled by bus or railroad, with only a few belongings.

Many travelled west to California to look for work as migrant fruit pickers. The brutal treatment some of them received was later described in John Steinbeck's novel *The Grapes of Wrath*.

In Germany Hitler attempted to turn the Berlin Olympic Games into a huge propaganda exercise for his racist Nazi regime. He was furious when brilliant black athlete Jesse Owens won the gold medals for sprint events and broke the record for the long jump; Hitler refused to congratulate him.

Popular illustrator Norman Rockwell's homely scenes of Middle America regularly appeared on the cover of the *Saturday Evening Post*.

Life magazine, with news and human interest stories, was started in the USA.

British publisher Allen Lane had started Penguin Books, an affordable list of quality paperback fiction priced at sixpence (5p) a copy. Non-fiction Pelican Books soon followed, and the children's list Puffin was launched in 1941.

An exciting new penguin pool, designed by Lubetkin and Tecton, was opened at London Zoo.

I n America, as the Depression forced families from their homes to look for work, children of migrants were unable to attend school. Millions were forced to abandon their education, and many took to the roads on their own.

At home in Britain, I read about girls' boarding schools in stories featuring sporty, outgoing heroines. Fortunately I managed to avoid the reality: I was cared for at home by my mother and Nelly, our easy-going teenage 'mother's help', and attended the local high school. But other powerful influences were now at work on children: in the USA they were identified as having a huge commercial potential. Clothes, toys and other merchandise were tied in to appealing characters. Vast fortunes were created by the 'Kings of Chocolate' like Forrest Mars and Milton Hershey, and by the Wrigley chewing-gum company. By the age of seven the Hollywood child star, ringleted, dimpled Shirley Temple, had sung and tap-danced her way with almost uncanny charm and professionalism to world adulation. She was not only a child fashion icon; she also helped people to forget for a little while both the Depression and the grim forces on the march in Europe.

In dancing classes and stage schools worldwide many young hopefuls were attempting to follow in the footsteps of little Shirley Temple.

Unaccompanied children eagerly packed the cinemas for special Saturday morning film shows. (In Britain, admission 1 penny.)

Some homes introduced a serving hatch between kitchen and dining room. It eased the servant problem but was isolating for the housewife.

Space-saving one-room flats were on show in London. Service flats where meals and cleaning services could be ordered up suited professional city dwellers everywhere.

French architect Charles-Édouard Jeanneret, known as 'Le Corbusier' ('The Crow'), led the new, clear-cut, functional 'International Style', dubbed 'machines for living'.

Last orders – A roadhouse in the Midwest, USA – 1938

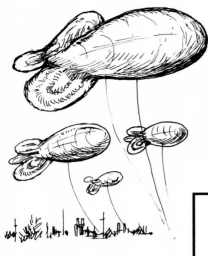

Preparation for air defence included searchlights, barrage balloons and anti-aircraft guns.

Gas masks were hot and uncomfortable to wear for any length of time.

Many Basque refugee children were evacuated to Britain, cared for by volunteers.

In his painting *Guernica*, Spanish artist Pablo Picasso depicted the horror of the bombing of that Basque city in 1937 by German aircraft supporting Franco's rebels.

Franco's Fascist forces were winning in Spain.

R. D. Russell's veneered wood console TV set was viewed through a mirror set into the underside of the cover.

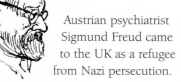

Austrian psychiatrist Sigmund Freud came to the UK as a refugee from Nazi persecution.

Sandbags were piled outside the entrances to buildings as a protection against bomb blast.

1938

War in Europe was expected at any time. Hitler was demanding that Czechoslovakia hand over the Sudetenland, a mountainous border area with a large German population. The Czechs were prepared to fight and looked to France and Britain as allies.

At home air-raid shelters were hurriedly dug, army reserves were called up and barrage balloons, the large inflatables designed to repel enemy aircraft, appeared in the sky around our cities. We school children tried on our gas masks and did air-raid drill.

But in September British prime minister Neville Chamberlain flew to Munich to meet Hitler, Mussolini and the French prime minister to try to avoid a war. They agreed that the Sudetenland should be handed to Germany and in return Hitler agreed not to make any more territorial demands. Chamberlain made a historic speech and many people, remembering the horrors of the First World War, agreed that war should be avoided at all costs.

The public practised air-raid drills, hurrying into the shelters when the warning sirens sounded.

Recruiting drives urged young men to join up. Older people were encouraged to train for voluntary war service on the Home Front.

Compulsory conscription for military service was resisted by the Liberal and Labour parties. (But introduced in 1939 for men between 18 and 41.)

In 1937 the airship *Hindenburg*, proud symbol of German aviation, had exploded while docking in New Jersey, USA. It immediately burst into flames and was destroyed in less than a minute, killing 35 passengers and crew.

British prime minister Chamberlain was cheered when he arrived back from the meeting in Munich. 'I believe it is peace for our time,' he said, waving the agreement with Hitler.

The popularity of jazz was giving way to the big, highly orchestrated 'swing' sound. In the USA star musicians like virtuoso clarinettist Benny Goodman toured with their bands playing to huge audiences.

Hollywood dancing partnership Fred Astaire and Ginger Rogers did a lot to lighten world gloom. They starred in *Shall We Dance?*, with music and lyrics by George and Ira Gershwin, released in 1937. George died of a brain tumour in that year aged 39.

Legendary blues singer Bessie Smith died in 1937 in a car crash.

Two of the greatest jazz vocalists ever, Ella Fitzgerald and Billie Holiday, were both making records.

24-year-old US boxer Joe Lewis triumphed in the fourth round against German champion Max Schmeling at New York's Yankee Stadium.

In Germany, on 12 November, Jewish shops were broken into and looted, synagogues burned and Jews beaten in the streets. This outrage, organized by the Nazis, was named *Kristallnacht* – 'Night of Broken Glass'.

At home in Britain we breathed a collective sigh of relief and returned to normal life. But refugees were arriving from Germany and Austria, where Jews were being deprived of all their rights as citizens, their businesses smashed and all political opposition brutally repressed. An escape route was arranged to bring Jewish children to Britain or America and place them in families.

Hitler's propaganda minister Joseph Goebbels knew how to manipulate the modern media to glorify the Nazi regime. At a spectacular rally in Nuremberg, designed to show German military might, Hitler addressed wildly enthusiastic followers. In the USA there was strong feeling against involvement in European affairs. President Roosevelt, intent on getting his 'New Deal' policies implemented, gave an assurance that America would not go to war unless attacked.

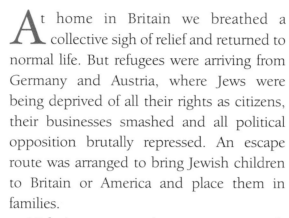

A fisherman near the Comoros Islands, off the coast of East Africa, caught a live coelacanth fish, thought to have been extinct for 70 million years.

Hitler's architect Albert Speer designed the stadium for the Nazi Nuremberg rally with full dramatic effect.

Many Jewish refugee children who had found sanctuary in Britain or America never saw their parents again.

Parisian hats were as frivolous as ever.

In Britain, the black bowler hat symbolized solid middle-class respectability.

The British working man stuck to his cloth cap.

The rolled-brim 'homburg' hat was for formal city wear.

The grey or brown 'trilby' hat was for every day.

A slice of bread by the roadside – Northern France – 1940

British children were evacuated from cities to homes in 'safe' areas in the countryside.

Many were bewildered and bitterly homesick. Some had returned home before the bombing started.

It was a time of heartbreaking goodbyes, as wives and parents saw their husbands and sons off to military service.

The new British prime minister, Winston Churchill, was an immensely charismatic figure who showed dogged determination, courage and optimism in the face of huge odds.

1940

In 1939 Hitler broke his promise not to seek more territory and invaded the rest of Czechoslovakia. The final flashpoint came when, triumphant that he had signed a non-aggression pact with Russia, he invaded Poland. Suddenly we were at war. We listened to the prime minister's announcement with a mixture of fear, resignation and bravado. As an all-female family we had no father or brothers to be called up into military service. We expected immediate air raids, perhaps poison gas. But for the rest of that year no attack came.

That winter, Hitler's troops invaded Denmark and Norway. In May 1940 Winston Churchill succeeded Chamberlain as British prime minister. On the day he took office, Germany invaded France, Holland, Belgium and Luxembourg. Churchill made no optimistic promises. He offered only 'blood, toil, tears and sweat' before victory could be accomplished.

As the German army advanced, French refugees took to the roads in cars, wagons and pushcarts, taking with them what belongings they could. They were machine-gunned by German aircraft.

After France had fallen the Free French forces rallied to General Charles de Gaulle, based in London. He broadcast to France via the BBC, urging resistance to German occupation.

Nightly blackouts were strictly enforced. Householders were fined if they showed a chink of light.

Air-raid wardens scanned the night sky from rooftops for approaching enemy aircraft.

Signposts and railway station names were removed in order to confuse enemy troops in case of invasion.

There was no street lighting. Petrol was available for essential journeys only.

Disgraced Russian leader Leon Trotsky, in exile in Mexico, was assassinated with an ice-pick on Stalin's orders.

In Hollywood David O. Selznick's epic American Civil War movie *Gone with the Wind*, based on Margaret Mitchell's bestseller, won nine Oscars.

In munitions and aircraft factories all over Britain men and women worked round-the-clock shifts to supply the weapons so desperately needed by the forces.

Canteen workers played an important part in keeping up morale.

British and French troops crowded the chaotic beaches at Dunkirk. They were strafed by enemy gunfire as they waited to be rescued.

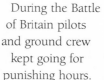

During the Battle of Britain pilots and ground crew kept going for punishing hours.

In Britain a million men aged between 15 and 65 volunteered for the Home Guard. 50% of them had served in the First World War. They were very poorly armed at first with old weapons and one rifle to every three men.

Zip-up, one-piece 'siren suits' were designed for warmth and could be put on quickly at any time of day or night.

Air-raid shelters, dug three feet into the ground in back gardens, saved many lives. Some people grew vegetables on the roof.

Ports and dock areas such as Liverpool, Tyneside and Glasgow were prime targets for German bombing.

Nazi troops poured into France across the Belgian and Luxembourg borders, bypassing the French defences (the so-called impregnable Maginot Line), pushing the allied armies northwards and cutting them off on the Normandy coast. By a miracle, small vessels of all kinds – sailing and fishing boats from England – managed to get close in shore at Dunkirk to assist the Royal Navy in transporting the men to safety. Nearly 200,000 British and 140,000 French troops were safely evacuated, though almost all their equipment was left behind.

The Germans entered Paris on 14 June and peace with France was signed. Germany now prepared to invade Britain. But it was decided that the Royal Air Force should first be destroyed and an air attack was launched. German confidence was misplaced. The 'Battle of Britain' was heroically fought in the sky over southern England and won by RAF pilots flying Spitfires and Hurricanes. They managed to destroy over half the attacking German aircraft. That autumn the Germans turned their attention to the relentless bombing of British cities, called the 'Blitz'.

Radar stations, which gave early warning to ground control of approaching enemy aircraft, were constantly under fire.

One Battle of Britain pilot in ten was Polish, fighting with the exiled Free Polish Air Force.

During the Blitz, air-raid wardens and ambulance teams worked to the point of exhaustion trying to rescue people from the rubble. Many were volunteers doing other jobs by day.

The Blitz on London was relentless. Londoners slept in air-raid shelters, cellars and on the platforms of underground stations.

As buildings blazed, firemen fought the flames all night amongst falling wreckage.

Lunch in the canteen – Los Angeles, USA – 1942

The Japanese made a surprise attack on Singapore through the jungle. There was panic as people crowded the docks, attempting to escape by sea.

Now in Burma, the Japanese threatened British India. Jungle warfare was something for which the Japanese troops were far better suited than their opponents.

Hitler arrogantly boasted that his troops would triumph in Russia before the winter began. He was wrong. The Russian army was very well led and fought back heroically.

Ignoring international law, the Japanese put their prisoners into forced labour camps to build roads and railways in appalling jungle conditions, on starvation rations.

In the USA a huge workforce of men and women was now employed at good wages manufacturing munitions and building battleships. Innocent American citizens of Japanese origin were rounded up and sent to detention centres. Their guards were instructed to shoot anyone trying to escape.

Women soldiers of the Red Army fought in armed combat alongside the men.

1942

America had now entered the war. In December 1941 Japan attacked and crippled the US Pacific Fleet at Pearl Harbor, Hawaii, and America joined the conflict on the Allied side. Japanese forces captured Rangoon and Singapore and carried the war with the Allies into Burma. Now they were fighting the US forces in the Pacific.

Hitler had turned on Russia, launching a huge attack involving half his armed forces. But he had underrated the savage Russian winter. The Soviets were accustomed to freezing conditions, but the German troops were without the proper warm clothing and the engines of their tanks froze. The Russians threw themselves into an epic struggle, their 'Great Patriotic War'. The British were fighting German and Italian forces in the Western Desert of North Africa. Driven back as far east as Egypt, they made a stand at El Alamein under General Montgomery and succeeded in turning the tide and driving the enemy back.

Russian composer Dmitri Shostakovich composed the first three movements of his seventh symphony, the 'Leningrad', while he was living in that besieged city under German attack. The siege lasted 890 days. When the city was liberated in 1944 about 200,000 inhabitants had been killed by shells and 630,000 had died of cold or starvation.

British general Montgomery's spirited leadership put fresh courage into the Eighth Army when they faced German general Rommel's Afrika Corps at El Alamein in Egypt.

British poet W. H. Auden used vividly expressive images. He was anti-war and deeply concerned with social issues.

He left England for America in 1939 and did not return until 1972.

US general Dwight Eisenhower took command of US forces in Europe based in London.

In Germany and Poland the Nazis had now unleashed a cold-blooded, systematic mass murder of Jewish and other prisoners in concentration camps.

The German hit song 'Lili Marlene' was sung by soldiers on both sides.

The transatlantic convoys were Britain's lifeline. Men of the merchant navy served bravely on unarmed ships, with heavy loss of life and vessels.

Between 1941 and 1943, at Bletchley Park in Britain, a brilliant team of male and female mathematicians managed to decipher the top secret German 'Enigma' code.

They used the first electronic computer, 'the Colossus'. (It filled an entire room and made a loud rattling noise.) This was a crucial turning point in the fight against the U-boat threat and saved many thousands of lives.

Ration books and queues were a part of life in Britain. Meat, cheese, sugar, eggs, sweets, butter, coffee, tea and jam were all rationed.

US servicemen were called 'GIs' because all their equipment was stamped 'GENERAL ISSUE'.

The new craze for 'Jitterbug' dancing was extremely strenuous. The GIs brought it to Britain, where teenagers were learning it fast.

We became accustomed to bombing. I slept under the stairs, though my mother preferred to risk staying in her own bed. Thanks to a fair and carefully worked-out rationing system we were not starving – in fact, we were very healthy – but we queued endlessly for food, and luxuries of any kind were a rare treat. You were not allowed more than 4 inches of hot water in your bath and holidays were out of the question. Older school children were expected to help with the war effort.

The USA was supplying armaments for the Allied war effort, transported mainly by sea. But this was a perilous undertaking as 'wolf packs' of German U-boats (submarines) in the Atlantic were taking a terrible toll on lives and shipping. For us at home, life dragged on drearily. Then American forces – the 'GIs' – began arriving, many encamped around Liverpool. To us they seemed to have stepped out of a Hollywood movie, wolf-whistling at local girls and awash with rare items such as chocolate bars and nylon stockings.

Cigarettes were scarce and pubs often ran out of beer.

Nothing could be wasted. Scraps were used to feed pigs.

Children collected scrap iron, aluminium kettles and saucepans to be made (we were told) into Spitfires.

American trombonist Glenn Miller and his band were top favourites.

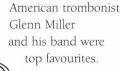

Nylon stockings were scarce and very precious. Women were driven to painting their legs to resemble stockings, complete with pencilled-on seams.

Some courageous women worked alongside men as secret Allied agents in German-occupied countries, helping the underground Resistance. They sent back coded wireless messages, knowing that if they were caught they would be sent to prison camps or shot, like Violette Szabo.

Odette Churchill was one of the secret agents who managed to survive. She and her husband Peter were captured and sent to concentration camps. They allowed the Germans to believe that they were related to Winston Churchill, which may have helped them to escape execution.

Childless women over 18 who were not doing vital war work joined the armed forces, where they played important roles as drivers, mechanics and radio and radar operators.

A last cup of tea – A railway station, Britain – 1944

On 6 June 1,000,000 Allied troops, American, British and Canadian, landed on the beaches of German-occupied Normandy.
There was fierce fighting.
Allied parachute troops had already landed.

There was massive air and naval cover. The heaviest resistance was at a beach codenamed 'Omaha', where there were 3,000 Allied casualties, mostly American. War photographer Robert Capa was aboard one of the landing craft. Supplies and reinforcements were brought in via the prefabricated floating docks, named 'Mulberry Harbour', a superb feat of military engineering.

British war artist Edward Ardizzone arrived in Normandy on 12 June and immediately began to record the scene in his sketchbook.
Another war artist, Stanley Spencer, was drawing Glasgow steelworkers building battleships.

Lovely singing and dancing star Betty Grable was the No. 1 pin-up of the US forces serving abroad.

1944

The cinema played an enormous part in our lives in this pre-television era. It was an oasis of glamour and an escape from a grey and often frightening reality. One of my older sisters had joined the WRNS (Women's Royal Naval Service). The other, now a young war bride with a husband serving in Burma, was living at home and working as an auxiliary nurse.

At least once a week, or twice if we could manage it, she and I sat in the local cinema watching romantic Hollywood movies like *Casablanca* and *Now, Voyager*. If the air-raid siren sounded we sat tight while the projectionist played the film over again until the all-clear sounded.

On heavily censored newsreels we watched Russian victories and the advance of Allied armies in Italy, where they had landed in 1943. And in June we saw the Allied invasion of northern France. To keep up morale, very little of the horrific bloodshed was shown.

In August Paris was liberated after four years of Nazi occupation. General de Gaulle marched down the Champs Elysées among cheering crowds.

A bitter revenge was taken by fellow countrymen against French people who had collaborated with the Nazis.

Hitler had wanted Paris to be destroyed but it was saved by General von Cholitz, commander of the city, who, defying orders, surrendered it undamaged.

In Germany Field Marshal Erwin Rommel took part in a failed plot to kill Hitler.

He committed suicide rather than face the consequences.

Young American singing star Frank Sinatra was adored by 'bobbysoxers' – teenage girls wearing white ankle socks.

Now in Poland, the Russian troops neared the capital Warsaw where, believing help was at hand, the Resistance rose up against the occupying Nazis. The Russian troops held back on the orders of Stalin. After almost suicidal heroism the rebels were forced to surrender. Over 200,000 people lost their lives.

Advancing on the Eastern Front the Red Army recovered Stalingrad, Smolensk and Kiev and now, at last, the siege of Leningrad was ended.

The Russian advance was pitiless. Thousands of German prisoners were taken. Many never returned home.

In the Italian campaign, Indian troops fought with the Allied forces in a bitter battle to capture the ancient but strategically vital monastery at Monte Cassino.

The Americans, ignoring orders from British overall command, were determined to be the first to enter Rome.

Luckily, this historic capital had been declared an 'open city' and was spared the ravages of war.

The conflict between the USA and Japan in the Pacific was hard, long-drawn-out and bloody. US soldiers and marines fought their way, island by island, towards Japan, facing an enemy who preferred death to the shame of being taken prisoner.

In India pressure was mounting from leader Mahatma Gandhi, the Congress Party (led by Jawaharlal Nehru) and the Muslim League (led by Mohammed Jinnah) for complete independence from British colonial rule.

From Poland, France and other Nazi-occupied countries people had been sent into forced labour in Germany. They were considered expendable and starved or worked to death.

In Britain food was scarce in spite of rationing. Parks, playgrounds and roadside verges were ploughed up to grow vegetables. German and Italian prisoners of war did farm work alongside the Women's Land Army.

The war seemed to be going well for the Allies at last. The exact time and place of the landings in France had, of course, been kept top secret. But we knew something big was about to happen. Rumours were rife. Troops were on the move everywhere. Many girls had fallen in love with service men stationed locally and now there were some sad goodbyes.

We were fortunate in being out of range of Hitler's new weapon, the V1 'flying bomb', a pilot-less winged weapon with a jet engine which cut out after a certain point, delivering one ton of high explosive. In wartime emotions run high, but are also strangely simplified. Most people just accepted the relentless bombing of German cities from British and US air force bases in East Anglia on a tit-for-tat basis. But there were those who, on religious or moral grounds, refused to carry arms. Some were drafted to work in the coalmines, others served as ambulance drivers or in army medical teams.

Due to Hitler's persecution of the Jews, many highly intelligent scientists, the brilliant physicist Albert Einstein among them, had taken refuge in the USA. In Britain and the US the race was now on against German scientists to develop the atomic bomb.

In Germany Wernher von Braun was responsible for overseeing the deadly V1 and V2 rocket missiles. After the war he and other rocket scientists went to America to work on the US space programme.

One of America's greatest popular composers and lyricists Cole Porter wrote probably the best and saddest song of the war, 'Every Time We Say Goodbye'.

Clothing was rationed and designed to save material: straight, unpleated skirts, no pockets, no turn-ups on trousers. Military-style square shoulders were fashionable.

Famous movie stars, theatre companies, dance bands and comedians toured the war zones to keep up forces' morale.

Most city art galleries and museums were closed, but string quartets and symphony orchestras performed regularly.

Supper alone – University town, Britain – 1946

Married men with children were the first to be released from military service.

Every ex-service man was given a 'gratuity' (a lump sum of money) and a complete outfit of clothes which included a choice of 'de-mob' (de-mobilization) suit.

Many ex-service men and women were returning home to full-time education. They had grants to study for degrees or professional qualifications.

Sir William Beveridge's plans for a welfare state were being implemented. There was now more support for the sick and unemployed.

British football was enjoying a huge post-war revival, with heroes like striker Stanley Matthews.

To relieve the housing crisis, pre-fabricated, one-storey homes with two bedrooms were designed to be assembled speedily on-site.

Of the 60,000 houses built in Britain between 1945 and 1946 two-thirds were 'pre-fabs'.

Only a lucky few couples got to the top of the waiting lists for a brand-new, low-rent council flat.

Others were reduced to living with parents or squatting in disused army camps.

In Britain the devastatingly cold winter of 1946–7 was followed by floods. Food and fuel shortages were worse than ever, and queues longer. The weekly meat and fat rations were well below wartime levels.

Many women, now coping with domestic life, missed the excitement and responsibility of the jobs they had done in wartime.

1946

In May 1945 peace had finally arrived in Europe; later, in August, Japan surrendered. It had been achieved at untold cost, culminating in the dropping of the terrible atomic bomb on Hiroshima, in Japan, and another on Nagasaki. The first explosion alone killed 80,000 people instantly, but it was the horrific, incalculable after-effects of its radiation that shocked the world. A destructive power had been unleashed that it was hard to face or understand.

The barbaric cruelty of the Nazi concentration camps and the murder of 6 million Jews had been revealed and had cast a shadow over the whole century. Hitler and Mussolini were dead: Hitler committed suicide and Mussolini was killed by Italian partisans; 21 top Nazis were tried and sentenced at Nuremberg. Now the rift between the opposing political ideologies of the western democracies and their former ally the USSR was becoming evident. Winston Churchill warned of an 'Iron Curtain' descending over Europe.

'GI brides' – British girls who had married US service men – were departing to a land of plenty.

Petrol shortages made transport difficult, but there were always bicycles.

Paris fashions returned to a softer, more feminine look with tiny waists. The military style was out, curves were definitely in!

The American 'zoot suit', with its widely padded shoulders, worn with a broad-brimmed hat, was fashionable (though considered rather flashy!).

Street hawkers who sold black market nylons and other goods illegally were called 'Spivs'.

In Paris young intellectuals gathered in cafés in the Bohemian quarter, St Germain-des-Prés, to dance and listen to jazz or the songs of Juliette Gréco.

They eagerly discussed the movies of Jean Cocteau and the novels of Jean-Paul Sartre.

The powerful, heartfelt singing voice of tiny, waiflike Edith Piaf made her a hugely popular icon of post-war France.

The publication of *Deaths and Entrances* by Welsh poet Dylan Thomas set him on the road to fame.

Another British novelist, George Orwell, showed his hatred of Communism in his satirical novel *Animal Farm*.

Graham Greene had emerged as a major British novelist in the 1930s. His Roman Catholicism was a recurrent theme in his work.

All over Europe there were thousands of orphaned children and 'displaced persons', some in camps, some wandering among the ruins searching for lost relatives.

Churchill was no longer Britain's prime minister. In the 1945 general election the Labour Party, led by Clement Atlee, had a clear majority. Ex-service men and women were returning to a Britain that had been exhausted by the war. Food and resources were even scarcer than in wartime. Industry was run down and there was a chronic housing shortage.

Yet, curiously, for the young it was a time of hope. We really thought that our old class-ridden society would change, and that under the Welfare State we would have a fairer Britain, with better social security, education and health care.

The USA had prospered from the boom in armaments production and people returned to a more affluent peacetime. They did not want the devastation of Europe to lead to the inflation and poverty that had followed the First World War. Harry Truman had become president following the death of Roosevelt in 1945.

The wreckage and devastation caused by the war was on an unprecedented scale.

Transport systems, factories, homes, schools, churches and hospitals all needed to be rebuilt.

Unexploded bombs were still being discovered and de-fused. In Britain over 50,000 were found.

Britain had escaped invasion but had used up her overseas assets to pay for the war. A huge export drive was needed.

Following the Japanese surrender of the former French colony Vietnam in 1945, Communist leader Ho Chi Minh (who had been armed by the Americans) took control.

The political map of Europe was again being re-drawn. The new 'Big Three', US president Harry Truman, British prime minister Clement Atlee and Soviet leader Stalin met at Potsdam in 1945 to discuss post-war boundaries.

The war had taken by far its greatest toll in the USSR. 20 million Russians lost their lives.

The US military conducted the first underwater atomic test off Bikini Atoll in the South Pacific.

The bikini, a minimal two-piece bathing suit, was named after the explosion and caused a sensation in Paris.

A potentially disastrous plan to split Palestine into separate Jewish and Arab states was proposed by Britain and the USA. Jewish settlers from all over the world now regarded Palestine as their homeland.

Food from the sky – Berlin – 1948

India had achieved independence in 1947, when the British viceroy, Lord Mountbatten, handed over power to a country split between Muslim and Hindu communities.

Fierce fighting between the two broke out almost immediately.

India's great spiritual leader, Mahatma Gandhi, was assassinated by a Hindu fanatic.

Thousands of mourners gathered to see his ashes cast into the river Jumna.

Yugoslav Communist leader Marshal Tito was determined to keep independence from Russian influence.

US poet T. S. Eliot, who wrote *The Wasteland* and had long resided in Britain, was awarded the Nobel Prize for literature.

Princess Elizabeth, heir to the British throne and now married to the Duke of Edinburgh, gave birth to their eldest son, Prince Charles. (She was crowned Queen Elizabeth II in 1953.)

In spite of clothes rationing, British high society still managed to turn out beautifully dressed for Ascot and the Buckingham Palace Garden Party.

Free milk was now available to all British school children.

1948

Germany, like the rest of Europe, was now divided into the Communist East and the democratic West. The capital city Berlin, although in East Germany, had a western zone controlled by the Allies. Then came the first crisis of the Cold War. In June the Russians cut all the road and rail supply lines to the western zone. The Allies responded by organizing a massive airlift to the 2.5 million people living in West Berlin, now effectively an island in East Germany. US aircraft, which had a short time before been dropping bombs on the city, ferried in food, coal, petrol and essential supplies of all kinds, until Stalin at last agreed to lift the blockade.

The city was later completely divided by a wall between eastern and western zones. It came to symbolize the gulf between life in the West, which offered political freedom, and the iron determination of Communism, an ideology now backed by all the apparatus of a police state. The wall eventually came down in 1989, and Germany was reunified in 1990.

The cultural influence of America was strongly felt in Europe, with plays like Tennessee Williams's *A Streetcar Named Desire* and the publication of Norman Mailer's novel *The Naked and the Dead*.

The US 'action' painter Jackson Pollock worked without brushes, dripping paint directly onto a canvas fixed to the floor to create a sweepingly patterned surface.

The Italian film *Bicycle Thieves*, directed by Vittorio de Sica, the sad tale of a poor bill-poster and his son, was hailed as a masterpiece of post-war realist cinema.

In 1947 the diary of Anne Frank, a young Jewish girl who had been hiding with her family in Nazi-occupied Holland from 1942 to 1944, was published.

The Franks were betrayed and arrested, and Anne later died in a concentration camp. But her diary was published and became a symbol of innocence and courage in a time of pitiless oppression.

Irish playwright George Bernard Shaw was still, aged 94, the controversial and argumentative 'Grand Old Man' of drama.

In Palestine, as British troops departed, Jewish leaders Chaim Weizmann and David Ben-Gurion declared a new independent state of Israel.

The only hope for peace in the region was in Jews and Arabs agreeing common boundaries.

Britain's National Health Service came into operation, offering free medical treatment, hospital care and dentistry for all.

Paris dress designer Christian Dior's 'New Look' required a corseted waist, padded hips and high heels. Evening gowns were strapless with huge skirts.

The French were never happy with rationing and got rid of it as soon as possible.

The new social reforms were costly and, still in debt after the war, the British economy was in poor shape.

To save valuable foreign currency, holidays abroad for British citizens were restricted by a meagre spending allowance.

In Europe and the USA munitions factories now went over to manufacturing domestic machinery. Fridges and washing machines were widely advertised and available on hire purchase.

In South Africa Dr Daniel Malan, leader of the Afrikaner National Party, became prime minister. He wanted complete segregation of black and white people.

In the USA Jackie Robinson was the first black American to play in major league baseball since 1884.

At this point in my life, as an art student in Oxford, I was less occupied with the grim struggle between East and West than with how to achieve the New Look. This fashion, unveiled by Paris dress designer Christian Dior in 1947, required yards and yards of dress material for huge skirts worn over frilled petticoats. In Britain clothes, like most things we longed for, were still strictly rationed. We were being urged by our government to put everything into the export drive to ensure our economical survival.

We resorted to making skirts out of curtains and ball dresses out of ex-RAF white silk parachutes. The young ex-service men with whom we danced talked very little about their war. They wanted to forget it. As the post-atomic bomb generation, our serious concerns were with how to react to it politically. The long-term environmental effects of this catastrophic invention had, as yet, hardly occurred to us.

In the USA the first drive-in hamburger café was opened by Richard and Maurice McDonald.

Beautiful British actress Vivien Leigh starred in the romantic movie adaptation of Leo Tolstoy's novel *Anna Karenina*.

Her real-life husband Laurence Olivier, one of Britain's great classical actors, starred in a film of *Hamlet*, which he also directed.

The most popular shows of all were big American musicals like Oscar Hammerstein II and Richard Rodgers' *Oklahoma!*

Britain held the Olympic Games in London and won six gold medals. It was the first Games ever televised.

Europe was hastily rebuilding its cities. High-rise blocks seemed like an economical solution, but some cheap, poorly designed housing schemes became the slums of the future.

Many people went to the cinema once a week, but an increasing number preferred to stay at home and watch television.

Ice cream sundaes – USA – 1950

The USA was doing an enormous amount to help economic recovery in Western Europe, with loans of $17 billion under the Marshal Plan.

Not all US citizens were enjoying affluence.

President Truman received an enraged response from the southern states when he appointed a Civil Rights Commission and called for an end to segregation of blacks and whites on public transport and in the military.

When Communist North Korea invaded the Republic of South Korea, Communist China backed the north. Refugees fled southwards.

United Nations forces, mostly American and British, were sent to support South Korea, led by controversial US general Douglas MacArthur.

As Chinese forces poured in from the north a war developed which lasted until 1953.

Fear of Communism increased when scientist Klaus Fuchs was found to have passed vital secrets to the USSR.

In the USA bullying senator Joe McCarthy was stirring up an atmosphere of distrust and suspicion. Some Americans were being required to denounce their colleagues as Communist supporters or else lose their jobs.

Playwright Arthur Miller won the Pulitzer Prize for his play *Death of a Salesman*.

He was later called before the House Committee on UnAmerican Activities, accused of Communist sympathies, but refused to give names of other possible suspects.

The latest American car designs were heavy on fuel and featured lots of chrome and 'tail fins'.

1950

There is a wide gulf between the lives of the prosperous American teenagers in my 1950 picture and the servant hard at work in a London basement in 1900. Following the Second World War the USA had become a great superpower, the wealthiest country in the world. These teenagers were surrounded by diversions, tempted by a high-powered advertising industry to buy luxuries of all kinds. But their black fellow citizens could not enter that soda bar and expect to be served.

The fear of Communism cast a cold shadow in the West. In 1949 the Chinese Communist leader Mao Zedong had proclaimed the New People's Republic, based on a Soviet model. The USA had the atomic bomb, and had used it, but the USSR was now conducting nuclear tests. Both countries operated extensive spy systems. In some areas of American life, fear of Communist sympathizers was on the verge of hysteria.

In China the long civil war was ended.

Mao Zedong, son of peasants, seized control when the USA stopped military aid to the nationalists.

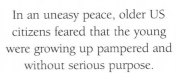

In an uneasy peace, older US citizens feared that the young were growing up pampered and without serious purpose.

Stalin ruled the USSR with an iron hand. He had become obsessed by his own glory and power.

His secret police ruthlessly repressed all opposition, and political prisoners were executed or sent to slave labour camps in the freezing wilderness of Siberia.

In a dramatic trial in the USA Alger Hiss, who had worked in the State Department, was tried for spying for the Soviet Union.

A young black American, Martin Luther King Jnr, who was studying to be a Baptist preacher, became passionately determined to challenge racism in his own country.

He was inspired by the teachings of Indian leader Mahatma Gandhi, who brought about political change by non-violent action.

Paris was still the centre of fashion, but designers like Dior were increasingly recognizing the importance of having a mass market for their clothes.

American teenagers were rejecting high fashion in favour of blue jeans, which have been worn all over the world ever since.

French dancer Zizi Jeanmaire's short, feathered haircut set a new fashion.

The old nineteenth-century European colonial powers like France, Holland, Britain, Belgium and Portugal were swiftly losing their empires, as African and far eastern countries followed India into independence.

Many British subjects from former colonies who were arriving to work and study in the UK regarded it as the 'mother country' and were English speaking.

The first human kidney transplant was performed by US surgeon R. A. Lawler.

French philosopher and novelist Simone de Beauvoir published her influential two-volume study of women, *The Second Sex*.

'Paddipads', the first disposable nappies, were now available.

But most mothers still washed out towelling nappies and hung them out to dry.

Two young movie actresses, Elizabeth Taylor and Audrey Hepburn, were having a big influence on how every girl wanted to look.

Dr Konrad Adenauer was now the first chancellor of the Federal Republic of Germany.

A steady flow of Germans were attempting to cross the border from Soviet-dominated East into West Germany.

British film director Carol Reed's black and white movie thriller *The Third Man*, with a script by Graham Greene, was set in occupied, war-damaged Vienna.

Starring Orson Welles and with Anton Karas's electrifying zither soundtrack, it became one of the most popular movies of its time.

The western European countries and the USA had formed a military alliance against possible Soviet attack, the North Atlantic Treaty Organization (NATO).

Computers had not yet revolutionized our lives, but two US engineers, John Eckert and John Mauchly, were about to invent the most advanced machine yet, the Universal Automatic Computer.

More British people took holidays abroad, but the majority still stuck to the pleasures of a pint at their local pub and braved the uncertain weather of the British seaside.

At this halfway point in the twentieth century I was living in London, attempting to launch myself into a career as a freelance illustrator. Marriage and children were soon to come. The contrast between the way my mother had run a home, which she did throughout two world wars, and my own imminent struggle to balance domesticity and motherhood with a passionate desire to draw was enormous.

Anyone who had lived through the last 50 years had experienced a rollercoaster of social change. There were more scientific and technical advances and innovation in the arts and communication than at any other period in history. Social upheavals were on the way. We lived in fear of atomic world war, but in spite of some major conflicts none came. And, as we pushed our unwieldy prams around the park, we saw rosy-cheeked children who were protected by immunization and penicillin against many of the life-threatening diseases that had so terrified my mother's generation. It was an encouraging and hopeful sight.

The End

Postscript: a breakfast shared – any big city, any time

The colour illustrations in this book were
done in gouache colour and chalk and
finished with fine brushes. All the
characters in them are imaginary.